Vicky was intensely curious about this unknown man who had fathered her children.

She moved closer to the mansion door to get a better look at him.

And he was definitely worth a second look.

Vicky frowned as an unexpected and totally unwelcome prickle of awareness danced over her skin.

James Thayer looked annoyed. Probably about her arrival. He certainly hadn't wanted her anywhere near the twins.

But she didn't care what he wanted.

She was the mother of six-month-old twins. No matter how forceful or formidable the handsome James Thayer might be, no matter how she might have to deceive him, she had a right to see her children.

A right to love them.

Dear Reader,

Spend your rainy March days with us! Put on a pot of tea (or some iced tea if you're in that mood), grab a snuggly blanket and settle in for a day of head-to-toe-warming—guaranteed by reading a Silhouette Romance novel!

Seeing double lately? This month's twin treats include *Her Secret Children* (#1648) by Judith McWilliams, in which our heroine discovers her frozen eggs have been stolen—and falls for her babies' father! Then, in Susan Meier's *The Tycoon's Double Trouble* (#1650), her second DAYCARE DADS title, widower Troy Cramer gets help raising his precocious daughters from an officer of the law—who also threatens his heart....

You might think of giving your heart a workout with some of our other Romance titles. In *Protecting the Princess* (#1649) by Patricia Forsythe, a bodyguard gets a royal makeover when he poses as the princess's fiancé. Meanwhile, the hero of Cynthia Rutledge's *Kiss Me, Kaitlyn* (#1651) undergoes a "make*under*" to conceal he's the company's wealthy boss. In Holly Jacobs's *A Day Late and a Bride Short* (#1653), a fake engagement starts feeling like the real thing. And while the marriage isn't pretend in Sue Swift's *In the Sheikh's Arms* (#1652), the hero never intended to fall in love, not when the union was for revenge!

Be sure to come back next month for more emotion-filled love stories from Silhouette Romance. I know I can't wait!

Mary-Theresa Hussey

Mary-Theresa Hussey
Senior Editor

Please address questions and book requests to:
Silhouette Reader Service
U.S.: 3010 Walden Ave., P.O. Box 1325, Buffalo, NY 14269
Canadian: P.O. Box 609, Fort Erie, Ont. L2A 5X3

Her Secret Children

JUDITH McWILLIAMS

SILHOUETTE *Romance*®

Published by Silhouette Books

America's Publisher of Contemporary Romance

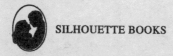

SILHOUETTE BOOKS

ISBN 0-373-19648-2

HER SECRET CHILDREN

Visit Silhouette at www.eHarlequin.com

Printed in U.S.A.

JUDITH McWILLIAMS

began to enjoy romances while in search of the proverbial "happily-ever-after." But she always found herself rewriting the endings, and eventually the beginnings, of the books she read. Then her husband finally suggested that she write novels of her own, and she's been doing so ever since. An ex-teacher with four children, Judith has traveled the country extensively with her husband and has been greatly influenced by those experiences. But while not tending the garden or caring for family, Judith does what she enjoys most—writing. She has also written under the name Charlotte Hines.

Medwin & Medwin
Attorneys at Law

Dear Mrs. Sutton,

I am writing to you on the behalf of my client, the Westinger Clinic, which you and your late husband used in your unsuccessful attempts at in vitro fertilization.

The clinic informs me that during the course of a recent internal audit, it came to their attention that their former director, in an effort to help infertile couples become parents, occasionally released the stored eggs of clients to be used as donor eggs. While his goal was laudatory, the director neglected to obtain a written release from the women whose eggs were used.

In order to rectify the situation, I have enclosed two forms requiring your signature. The first indemnifies the clinic from any liability in this matter. The second is included on behalf of James Thayer, who has sole custody of the six-month-old twins born from your eggs. The document allows you to relinquish all claims to the children. I am sure you will agree that it is in the children's best interests to continue living with their father.

Sincerely,

Edgar Medwin
Attorney at Law

Chapter One

"Almost there, almost there," Vicky Sutton chanted the words like a prayer. A prayer in which hope, fear and excitement were hopelessly entangled.

Steering her small rental car around yet another of the narrow road's hairpin curves, she finally saw a straight stretch ahead and pressed down on the accelerator. The car leaped forward, seemingly as eager as she was to get to her destination.

She'd come so far. And not just in distance, although the miles between suburban Philadelphia and rural England were considerable. But those miles dwindled to nothing when compared to the mental journey she'd made in the past two weeks.

Starting from a point of shocked disbelief at the incredible news the fertility clinic's lawyer had so reluctantly given her, Vicky had worked her way through furious anger that anyone, particularly a trusted doctor, could have done such a despicable thing, to euphoric joy at the unintended results of his act. She'd finally ended up deeply mired in intense frustration as she'd waited for the lawyers to negotiate the ground rules for a situation that appeared to have no legal precedent.

And now, after two interminable weeks, she was about to realize her heart's desire. She was finally going to meet them.

Her slender fingers tightened nervously on the steering wheel as she remembered she was also going to meet someone else. Someone who not only didn't want to meet her, but who had expressly forbidden her to come. Someone who had only grudgingly agreed to meet with her lawyer, Ms. Lascoe, after Vicky had threatened him with a lawsuit.

Vicky shivered at the thought of how he was going to react when he found out that, at the last minute, Vicky had decided to come herself instead of sending Ms. Lascoe as they'd agreed.

It didn't matter, she told herself. James Edward Andrew William Thayer wasn't going to get his own way this time—something she suspected hadn't happened to him very often in his privileged life.

Vicky's breath caught in her throat as she rounded the next curve and saw the twelve-foot-high sandstone pillars that marked the entrance to her destination, Thayer House.

Slowing almost to a stop, she carefully turned the car onto the neatly graveled driveway.

In the distance she could see a sprawling, three-story mansion sitting atop a slight rise. It radiated a sense of age and power that she unexpectedly found intimidating.

By the time Vicky actually reached Thayer House, her heart was thumping so hard she felt light-headed. All she could think about were her children. Behind that elegant facade were the children she'd yearned for all her life. Children she'd given up all hope of ever having. Until two weeks ago, when her prayers for motherhood had been so improbably answered.

Abandoning the car in the driveway, Vicky hurried toward the house. She stumbled slightly on the first of the three broad, shallow steps in her haste to reach the gleaming black door.

Grabbing the shiny brass knocker, Vicky gave it a sharp rap and, when the door wasn't immediately answered, administered a second thump. An interminable minute later, the door swung open on well-oiled hinges to reveal a slightly overweight, middle-aged man in a black suit.

"Good afternoon, madam," he said. "May I help you?"

"Ye—" Vicky's voice, stretched thin by her nerves, snapped on the word. Taking a deep breath, she tried again. "Yes, I'm here to see Mr. Thayer. I'm Ms. Lascoe."

"Certainly, he is expecting you, Ms. Lascoe. Welcome to Thayer House."

The man opened the door wider, and Vicky stepped inside, surreptitiously searching the vast entrance hall for her children, even though she knew it was highly unlikely that six-month-old twins would be passing their time there.

"I am Beech, the butler," the man said.

He sounded like a character straight out of a P. G. Wodehouse novel, Vicky thought, swallowing the nervous giggle that bubbled up in her throat.

"You may wait for Mr. Thayer in the green drawing room. He asked to be paged as soon as you arrived."

Paged? Vicky examined the word. Somehow the

modern reference seemed out of place in this old house. Although she could definitely see the advantages of a pager in a place this big.

"This way, Ms. Lascoe." Beech started toward the back of the hall.

Vicky followed him on trembling legs, desperately trying to conceal her escalating nervousness. All that stood between her and her children now was James Thayer. Her lips firmed in grim determination. He didn't stand a chance. She'd deal with the devil himself for her children's sake. What was one overprivileged Englishman?

Beech pushed open the door to a large room filled with an eclectic collection of museum-quality Chippendale furniture and comfortably faded chintz. He gestured her inside.

"If you'll have a seat, Mr. Thayer will be with you shortly."

"Thank you." Vicky's voice came out on a squeak of suppressed emotion.

Fortunately, Beech didn't seem to notice. He merely gave her a majestic nod and left, closing the door quietly behind him.

Too nervous to sit still, Vicky walked over to the French doors that opened onto a flagstoned terrace and peered out at the lush green perfection of the meticulously tended lawn stretching in all directions. To her right was an elaborate rose garden, and in the distance she could see a long glass greenhouse with an onionlike dome perched on one end.

As Vicky watched, a man emerged from the greenhouse and started across the grass toward the house.

She tensed as she took in the proud tilt of his head

and the casual elegance of his clothes. He had to be the owner of all this magnificence.

Intensely curious about this unknown man who had fathered her children, Vicky moved closer to the French doors in order to get a better look at him.

And he was definitely worth a second look, she conceded. He moved with the coordinated grace of a seasoned athlete, and he looked…

Vicky frowned as an unexpected and totally unwelcome prickle of awareness danced over her skin.

His hair was a dark brown that seemed to trap the brilliant June sunlight, giving it a reddish gleam. She couldn't quite make out the color of his eyes because of the distance, but they appeared dark. Dark and impenetrable. As if they were full of secrets he wouldn't easily give up.

Vicky's gaze slipped lower, studying the unyielding line of his tightly compressed lips.

He looked annoyed about something. Probably her arrival, she admitted. He certainly hadn't wanted her here. He hadn't wanted her anywhere near the twins. But she didn't care what he wanted.

She wasn't going to be talked into disappearing from her children's life. Not now. Not ever. The twins were the only children she would probably ever have, and she was determined to be part of their life. An important part.

Vicky took a deep breath, trying to control her nervousness. She was not relishing the coming interview. Not only did she hate personal confrontations, but James Thayer's bearing exuded a strength of purpose that she found very daunting. She'd come herself instead of sending Ms. Lascoe, and he was not going to take the news well.

Vicky retreated further into the room as he neared the French doors, wanting to put some distance between them.

She watched with a feeling of inevitability as he pushed open the door and stepped inside.

Giving her a terse nod, he said, "Good afternoon, Ms. Lascoe."

His clipped English accent poured through her mind, unexpectedly dislodging old, half-forgotten memories. Memories of when she and her best friend had watched, enthralled, as Diana married her prince in a blaze of pageantry. Memories of the sense of anticipation Vicky had felt. As if anything were possible— if you loved someone enough.

But she wasn't a romantic adolescent anymore. Now she was an adult. An adult who had long since learned that childish daydreams were not real life.

James blinked as his eyes adjusted to the dim light in the room and then blinked again when he got a good look at the slender woman standing by the fireplace.

The instantaneous sense of recognition that swept over him caught him completely off guard. He felt as if someone he'd once deeply loved had come home to him. He wanted to sweep her into his arms and hold her so tightly that she couldn't ever disappear again.

It made no sense, he thought in confusion. Ms. Lascoe wasn't someone he had ever met, let alone loved. What she was a very real threat to his peace of mind and his children's emotional security. He knew that. Knew it beyond a shadow of a doubt.

Critically, James studied her, trying to find a reason for his irrational reaction.

Could it be her superficial resemblance to his exwife? he wondered. Ms. Lascoe's hair was a similar dark blond, although judging from the fairness of her skin, her coloring was natural and not due to the skill of a hairdresser as Romayne's had been.

His eyes dropped to her mouth, and he was immediately consumed with the desire to feel her lips beneath his. Fighting the unwanted compulsion, he dragged his gaze upward to discover the most fantastic pair of blue eyes he'd ever seen. Eyes full of awareness. And intelligence, he realized with a distinct sense of shock.

Was she intelligent enough to see how the sight of her had disconcerted him? The possibility made him uneasy. He hoped not. She might try to use his odd reaction against him in their negotiations.

James reached for her extended hand in the hope that social conventions would bring a sense of normalcy to their meeting.

Vicky trembled inwardly at the sensations which sparked to life as his hand closed over hers, adding a whole new dimension to the tension she already felt.

To her profound relief he immediately released her, and Vicky hurriedly stepped back. Sexual attraction was nothing more than an insidious trap, she reminded herself, unconsciously twisting the thin gold wedding band around her finger. Once before she'd allowed a physical reaction to override her good judgment and look where that had led.

"I'm looking forward to meeting the twins," Vicky threw into the tense silence.

"Yes, the twins," he repeated, and Vicky searched his impassive features for a clue to his thoughts.

Not that she really needed further confirmation that she was about as welcome in his home as an outbreak of foot-and-mouth disease, she thought wryly. Nor could she entirely blame him for his attitude. Not really. She might have been overjoyed to find that she was the mother of a set of six-month-old twins, but that same news must have been a devastating blow to him. To have a stranger suddenly appear and demand access to your children must be both frustrating and scary.

But as guilty as she felt about the upheaval she was undoubtedly causing in his life, his feelings were secondary to the fact that she was the children's biological mother. She had a right to see them. A right to love them and to influence their lives.

"It is my hope that once you see how well the twins are doing, you'll advise your client to drop her demands for access to them," he said.

Vicky briefly weighed telling him that not only was she Mrs. Sutton, but that nothing was ever going to make her go away and forget that she had two children. She decided against it. The news of her real identity would only make him mad. No, make him madder, she amended as she took in the corded muscles in his jaw. He might refuse to let her see the twins. She felt a brief flare of panic at the thought.

She'd tell him later, she thought. After she had seen her children.

"As the children's father—"

"Mrs. Sutton is the children's mother," Vicky inserted.

"Simply because she unknowingly contributed a couple of microscopic bits of genetic material—"

"Mary Rose and Edmond wouldn't exist without that contribution," Vicky countered, resisting the impulse to point out that his genetic contribution had been even smaller. Trying to score off him wasn't going to help the situation. And probably wasn't possible, she conceded. He didn't strike her as the kind of man who would ever admit, even to himself, that he had been bested.

"But I'm the one who has raised them," he insisted.

"Only because their mother had no idea they existed until two weeks ago!"

James felt a flash of guilt at the bleakness of her words. It wasn't his fault that Mrs. Sutton hadn't known about the twins. He hadn't been a party to the doctor's decision to illegally sell her frozen eggs, the ones Vicky had stored at his fertility clinic. James had honestly believed the eggs had been donated by an anonymous woman. He wasn't knowingly responsible for Mrs. Sutton's pain.

But he *would* be responsible if she caused his children pain with her demand for a role in their lives. A demand that he didn't understand. It could simply be that she was curious about them. Or her reason could be more ominous. She could have a hidden agenda. People usually did when there were large sums of money involved. And his children would inherit not only a great deal of money, but a social position at the top of the English aristocracy.

Mrs. Sutton could be planning to use her position as the twins' biological mother to enhance her own social and financial standing. Hell, Mrs. Sutton undoubtedly had an agenda that her lawyer had no clue about, he thought, as he studied the delicate lines of Ms. Lascoe's face. She certainly didn't look like any high-powered lawyer he'd ever met. What she looked like was an idealist. Someone who didn't deal with the real world much. Someone who still believed in fairy tales and happily-ever-after. Ms. Lascoe could well be projecting her own virtues and maternal instincts onto her client.

"You can hardly claim Mrs. Sutton has discovered an overwhelming love for two children she didn't even know existed a few weeks ago," he bit out, his frustration at not being able to get a handle on the situation showing.

"She's their mother," Vicky said.

"And I'm their father!"

"This discussion is becoming circular," Vicky said. "Allow me to assure you that Mrs. Sutton is not trying to usurp your role. Or your wife's come to that."

"Ex-wife. Romayne doesn't have a role in their lives. She remarried shortly after they were born and now lives in France. I have sole custody of the twins."

Vicky blinked at the unspoken "thank God" that hung in the air between them. She wished she had the right to ask a few questions, starting with how could any woman give birth to two children and then abandon them? So what if Romayne Thayer hadn't provided the eggs from which the twins had been conceived. She'd carried them for nine months. How could she just walk away from them?

For that matter how could Romayne have walked away from James Thayer? Vicky pondered the seemingly inexplicable circumstance. On the surface he appeared to have everything that any woman could possibly want in a husband. But then, looks could be deceptive. She of all people should know that.

She blocked off the flood of memories that cascaded through her. It was over. The past was dead and truly buried. Now was the time to keep her sights firmly fixed on the future.

"I'm here to assess the children's physical and emotional growth while I work out a shared custody arrangement with you." Vicky tried to use one of the techniques she'd learned for dealing with conflict, that of sounding both reasonable and confident. Unfortunately, she was very much afraid that it was going to take far more than one weekend workshop to give her the tools to deal successfully with James Thayer.

"Shared custody!" He bit the words off as if they were an obscenity.

"Why not?" Vicky forced herself not to retreat in the face of his anger. Trying to placate unreasonableness in the hopes of avoiding conflict didn't work. Her first marriage had taught her the utter futility of that approach.

"Mrs. Sutton is an American." James uttered the words as if they were a criminal indictment. "The twins are English. Someday Edmond will inherit this estate. He has to learn how to run it."

"Edmond is six months old. He has plenty of time to learn everything he needs to know."

"He needs to develop an affinity for the estate early, and he can't get that if Mrs. Sutton succeeds in dragging him off to America."

"My client is not suggesting he live in America permanently," Vicky said.

"Thank heavens for small favors," James muttered. "And would you please sit down so I can, too."

Vicky was caught off guard by the sudden change of subject.

"Certainly." She dropped onto an ornately carved Chippendale chair with an incongruously frayed needlepoint seat.

"Thank you," he said as he sat on the overstuffed

sofa across from her. "I have been thinking about a cover story for your visit."

"We could always just try the truth," she said, and was immediately engulfed in guilt when she remembered that her whole presence at Thayer House was a lie. But a necessary lie. And it wouldn't last long. Once she had seen the twins, she would tell Mr. Thayer the truth.

"People might not understand," he said.

People? Vicky examined the word. Or did he mean one person in particular? Did James have a new wife lined up? Was that who he was worried about misunderstanding her visit?

Vicky instinctively rejected the idea of his remarriage. But only because a stepmother might resent a child other than her own inheriting all this magnificence, she told herself.

"I have decided that we will say you are a distant relation from America who is tracing her family and are here to check our records.

"It's imperative that you not upset my great-aunt who lives with me. She's a bit…"

James paused as if searching for a word and finally settled on "…eccentric."

Eccentric? Vicky examined his choice, wondering what kind of behavior would be considered eccentric in a country that had spawned *Benny Hill* and *Monty Python's Flying Circus*. She didn't have a clue, not that it really mattered. She had no intention of upsetting his aunt if she could avoid it. And she fervently hoped that the woman would return the favor. All Vicky wanted was to see her children. The sooner the better.

"I will do my level best not to upset your aunt or anyone else in the house," Vicky assured him.

She was too late, James thought grimly. She'd already upset him. Just the sight of her had done that. And as for what her actual presence in his house might do to his peace of mind...

"Now that we've agreed to a cover story, may I see the children," Vicky demanded, her impatience getting the best of her.

"No, it won't be four for almost an hour."

"I thought midnight was the traditional witching hour. What's the significance of four?"

"That's when I see the twins. After their nap and before their dinner. Children do best on a schedule." He rattled off the words as if they'd been a lesson he'd memorized.

Vicky quashed the impulse to tell him exactly what she thought of such rigidity. Mainly because she didn't know if he really believed such drivel or if he was just using it to stall her.

"I'll—" Vicky broke off at the soft rap on the door.

"Come in," James called.

The door was immediately opened by Beech. "Herr Murchin has called, sir."

"Thank you, Beech. Tell him..." James paused and studied Vicky as if trying to decide what to do with her.

"Why don't I just go to the nursery while you're on the phone? I won't wake the children, and then I'll already be there when you come at four," Vicky tried, not really expecting him to agree.

He didn't.

"Nanny doesn't like the twins' routine to be upset," he said.

Stuff Nanny! Vicky thought on an uncharacteristic

flash of anger. They were her kids, and she didn't give a damn what some glorified baby-sitter thought.

"I'll take you to see them at four," James repeated, to Vicky's disappointment but not her surprise. Nanny seemed to have had things pretty much her own way. So far, Vicky thought. But things would be different now that she was here. No employee was going to dictate to her when she could see her own children.

"Beech—" James turned to the patiently waiting butler "—would you show Ms. Lascoe to the Chinese bedroom."

"Certainly, sir." Beech moved slightly to one side of the door, and Vicky, knowing that protesting further wouldn't do her any good, gave James a perfunctory nod and left.

She followed the silent butler back into the front entrance hall, up the ornately carved mahogany staircase and down a long hallway until he finally stopped in front of a set of double doors.

"Here we are, Ms. Lascoe, the Chinese bedroom," he announced as he flung the door open to reveal the biggest bedroom she had ever seen.

"The bath is through that door." Beech pointed to a smaller door on far the wall. If you should want anything, pick up the phone beside the bed and push *0*. It will connect you with the staff."

Staff? Just how many people constituted staff? Vicky wondered curiously. Thayer House seemed to be run more along the lines of a luxury hotel than a private dwelling.

"If I might have your key?"

"My key?" Vicky repeated blankly.

"To your car. Your luggage is in your car, I presume?"

That's where she'd left it all right, she thought as she rummaged in her purse for the key to the rental car. Along with whatever social acumen she'd ever possessed. There was something about this place that made her feel inadequate. As if everyone knew a set of rules she didn't.

And they undoubtedly did, she thought with an inward sigh.

Finally locating the key, she handed it to Beech who gave her an encouraging nod and left.

There had to be hundreds of social dos and don'ts associated with living in a place like this, she realized. Rules that differentiated those who belonged and those who were merely there on sufferance. Not that it mattered, Vicky thought, trying to bolster her flagging self-confidence. She wouldn't be around long enough for her ignorance to become an issue.

But her children would. This was her children's natural world, both by birth and by heritage. If they were going to thrive in it, they were going to have to know a lot of things she couldn't teach them.

Vicky sank into the pale green silk chaise longue beside the white marble fireplace, suddenly feeling overwhelmed by the task ahead of her. Why couldn't that blasted doctor who'd stolen her eggs have sold them to a nice middle-class couple? A couple whose lifestyle she could relate to. But James Thayer's lifestyle…

Her gaze swept the room, taking in the delicate beauty of its Regency mahogany furniture, the obvious age of the faded tapestry bed hangings and understated luxury of the thick Aubusson carpet on the floor. This was a completely alien world to her. A surge of depression washed through her, leaving a feeling of hopelessness in its wake as it ebbed.

Stop it. Vicky pulled herself up short. It didn't matter that James Thayer could provide a luxurious lifestyle for the twins. The basics a child needed were the same whether they lived in a palace in rural England or a crowded apartment in New York City. Kids needed the love and attention and personal involvement of their parents. That couldn't be bought *or* delegated to a nanny as James seemed to be doing. It had to come from the heart, and she was willing to give it.

Vicky stiffened at the tentative knock on the door. Now what, she wondered. Even as efficient as Beech appeared to be, there hadn't been time for him to get downstairs, retrieve her luggage and return. Unless he'd forgotten something and come back for it.

Maybe it was James Thayer. Maybe he had relented and was going to show her the children now instead of at four.

Jumping to her feet, Vicky rushed across the thick carpet and yanked open the door.

Chapter Two

Vicky stared at the person standing in the hallway just outside her door. It was neither James Thayer, as she'd hoped, nor the butler. Instead her visitor was a plump, elderly woman wearing a mauve dress that appeared to be composed of multiple layers of floating chiffon. Around her shoulders she had tied a gorgeous red silk shawl bordered with a twelve-inch fringe. Her thin white hair seemed to be straining away from her round face as if it were trying to escape.

Bemused, Vicky watched as the woman patted the waist-length strand of pearl-like beads. Every one of her short fingers boasted a ring with an oversize stone. It was the most colorful collection of costume jewelry Vicky had ever seen. Fake rubies vied with man-made emeralds and clashed with faux sapphires while the monstrous zircon on her little finger seemed to eye the display with total disdain.

"Who are you, gel?" The woman broke the silence. "Have I met you?"

"No," Vicky said, absolutely sure of the fact. She couldn't possibly have met this woman and failed to remember her. "I'm Vicky…" Her voice trailed away in dismay as she remembered that she was supposed to be Ms. Lascoe whose given name was Kathleen. One thing was becoming increasingly clear. She was not cut out to be a spy. It took a far better memory than she would ever have to keep track of all the lies that needed to be told.

So now what did she do? Try to convince the old woman she hadn't really said Vicky? No, too risky, she decided. Just because the woman was old didn't mean she was hard of hearing or easily confused. Vicky's best bet at this point would be to try to pass her name off as a nickname if James had noticed Ms. Lascoe's real first name.

"You got a last name, gel?" the woman demanded.

"Lascoe," Vicky compounded the lie. "And you are Ms.…"

"Ain't a Ms. I'm a lady."

"Well, yes, I hope I am, too," Vicky said, "but—"

"No, I mean my name is the Lady Sophronia Elizabeth Alberta Edwina Thayer."

"I am pleased to meet you, Lady Sophronia," Vicky said, trying to put their meeting on some kind of normal footing, although she was fast coming to the conclusion that normal and the Lady Sophronia were mutually incompatible terms.

"Call me Sophie. You a friend of James?" Sophie eyed her curiously. "What do they call it these days? A very good friend?"

Vicky's breath caught in her throat at the image Sophie's words evoked. Images of being held in James's arms. Her heart raced and she could almost feel the pressure of his arms tightening around her as he pulled her closer to him. His dark blue eyes were gleaming with desire. Desire for her. His firm lips were slightly tilted as if savoring the anticipation of kissing hers. His...

Get a grip, woman! Vicky determinedly hauled her imagination up short. The situation was already complicated enough without her falling prey to adolescent fantasies about James Thayer.

"We are not friends. Good or otherwise," Vicky said emphatically, as if her very vehemence could somehow extinguish her odd reaction to the man.

"Then why are you here?" Sophie asked.

"I'm a distant relative of the Thayer family from America, and I'm in England tracing my roots. Mr. Thayer is allowing me to visit while I do it," Vicky said, repeating the fiction James had devised.

"A family connection, eh?"

Sophie studied Vicky with an intensity she found unsettling. She wished she knew a little more about this surprising woman. Could she be the great-aunt James had warned Vicky against upsetting? Sophie certainly had all the hallmarks of being eccentric by anyone's standards.

"Since you're so interested in the family have you seen the newest additions?" Sophie asked. "Damned fine specimens, even if I do say so myself."

"No, but I'd love to see them." Vicky tried to sound no more than causally interested, even though her heart was beating so loudly she was sure Sophie could hear it.

Sophie pushed aside her shawl and twisted the pendent watch pinned to the bodice of her dress so she could check the time.

"Tea ain't for a few minutes yet, so I don't see why not. Course *she* may have a reason why not." Sophie gave an inelegant snort. "Got ideas above her station, that one does."

That one being the nanny? Vicky wondered, but she didn't ask. She didn't want Sophie to dwell on any possible objections for fear she would change her mind.

"Maybe she won't mind," Vicky tried.

Sophie pursed her lips together consideringly. "Guess it won't harm none to try."

Sophie turned with a swirl of draperies and marched toward the door.

"Come along, gel!" she threw over her shoulder. "Time and tide wait for no man."

"Coming." Vicky caught up with her in the hallway, feeling as if she were part of a cavalry charge.

After a ten-minute hike through the bowels of the house, Sophie finally stopped in front of a white painted door in a sunny corridor on the third floor.

"This is the nursery." Sophie hissed the information to Vicky out of the corner of her mouth. "Maybe *she* won't be here."

"We can only hope," Vicky muttered as Sophie turned the shiny brass knob and cautiously pushed open the door.

Vicky took a deep breath, trying to control the frantic pounding of her heart. She was so close. So close to actually seeing the children she'd never thought to have.

"May I help you, my lady?" The clipped voice made a mockery of the polite words.

Vicky looked up to find their entrance blocked by a woman in a spotless navy uniform.

Vicky scanned the large room behind her, but it was

empty. Wherever the children slept, they didn't do it in this room.

"We want to see Mary Rose and Edmond," Sophie said.

"That is not possible," Nanny decreed. "The twins are napping and mustn't be disturbed.

"We won't wake them." Vicky tried to be conciliatory when what she really wanted to do was shove the blasted woman out of the way and find her children.

"No." The woman delivered the emphatic negative a second before she closed the door in their faces.

"But…" Vicky found herself talking to the door.

"See what I mean about ideas above her station," Sophie muttered angrily. "But I promised, and I keep my promises.

What had Sophie promised and to whom had she promised it? Vicky wondered, wanting to scream in frustration at her lack of information about the whole situation.

"You wouldn't happen to know a curse I could use on her, would you?" Sophie unexpectedly asked.

"Sorry," Vicky said with real regret. As far as she was concerned, the nanny could only be improved by a curse or two.

"Pity. Guess we might as well go have tea."

"All right." Vicky dispiritedly trailed after Sophie. She felt almost sick with disappointment at having been so close, only to have been turned away.

"We always have our tea in the morning room," Sophie informed her as they crossed the main hallway. "Don't know why, since it's afternoon, but we ain't got an afternoon room."

"I should think this place has enough rooms for

every minute of the day,'' Vicky said. ''Why don't you just call one of them the afternoon room if you want?''

''You Americans have no sense of tradition!''

''We make up for it with common sense and practicality.''

''Practicality! Ha! And you without a curse to your name.''

Vicky followed Sophie into the morning room. It was a small room, relatively speaking, and had a cozy, welcoming air to it. The bright afternoon sunlight streamed through the south-facing windows, highlighting the blue-and-yellow chintz furniture. The pastel floral design in the Aubusson carpet added to the general feeling of warmth.

''Curses aren't very practical,'' Vicky pointed out as she tiredly dropped on the sofa. ''Even if they really worked, it might take years to get the result you wanted. If you want to get rid of someone, you should use more direct methods.''

Such as ''You're fired, Nanny,'' Vicky thought.

''I wish I could, but, unfortunately, the days when you could simply kill off people are over. Nowadays, everyone minds everyone else's business.''

''Not an entirely bad thing,'' James said as he entered the room. His gaze swung to the sofa to see to whom his aunt was speaking and found himself staring into a pair of bright blue eyes.

Vicky looked up at the sound of his voice and felt her mouth drying as the sight of James Thayer's leanly chiseled features filled her entire field of vision, immediately rendering everything else in the room unnoticeable. So her first disconcerting reaction to him hadn't been a fluke, she realized in dismay. For some reason the very sight of James Thayer put every one of her feminine instincts on red alert.

But why? she wondered, trying to understand her reaction in the hope of curing it. Granted, he was intriguingly handsome, but she hadn't been particularly susceptible to masculine good looks since she'd outgrown adolescent infatuations. And she'd never been impressed by either social standing or money. So what was it about James Thayer that made her so aware of him? Could it be because of the children they shared? It was certainly an odd enough circumstance to account for it. Hopefully, once she got used to the idea she'd be able to see him as just an ordinary man. If you could call being a wealthy English aristocrat and living in a historic house filled with gorgeous antiques ordinary, she thought ruefully.

"We were talking about getting rid of people, James, but unfortunately Vicky doesn't know any curses," Sophie said.

"Vicky?" James's dark brows drew together in a frown that made Vicky's stomach twist nervously. "I'm sure you signed your letters Kathleen Lascoe."

She might have known he was the kind of man to take a good look at the signature on any correspondence from a lawyer, Vicky thought in dismay. Well, there was nothing for it but to stall until she could get in to see her children.

"Vicky is a nickname I picked up when I was just a baby," she ad-libbed, praying that he hadn't somehow found out that the twins' biological mother was named Vicky. He might not have. All the correspondence from the fertility clinic had referred to her as Mrs. Zane Sutton, and she knew that the letters Ms.

Lascoe had sent him had also referred to her by her late husband's name.

Vicky felt the first twinges of a tension headache begin to build behind her eyes. Conspiracies were the very devil to keep afloat. Things would be much easier once she had a chance to see the twins and could confess her real identity.

Vicky looked into James's implacable features and felt a shiver of apprehension slither over her skin. And then again maybe things wouldn't. James Thayer was perfectly capable of ordering her off his property.

The arrival of the stately butler carrying a tray was a welcome interruption to her tortured thoughts.

"Ah, Beech, set the tea tray here." Sophie gestured toward the table in front of her.

"Lemon or milk in your tea, Vicky?" Sophie asked as she deftly poured.

"Milk, please," Vicky said, wishing it were coffee. Strong coffee. She'd feel more able to deal with the formidable James with a hefty dose of caffeine in her system.

Sophie handed the cup to James who ceremoniously handed it to Vicky. She accepted it, being careful not to touch him in the process. She didn't need any more distractions.

"Vicky says she's researching her roots," Sophie said with a quick glance at James.

Vicky held her breath, waiting for Sophie to mention the aborted trip to the nursery. To Vicky's relief, Sophie didn't.

"How does one search out one's roots, Vicky?" Sophie demanded.

Vicky hastily took a sip of tea while she tried to

think. "On the computer," she finally said. "In gene-
alogy banks."

"I believe one of the largest in the world is at the
Mormon church in Utah, Aunt Sophie," James said,
confirming Vicky's suspicion that Sophie was his aunt.

"Really, dear boy?" Sophie gave him a thoughtful
look that made Vicky uneasy.

Was Sophie really as flighty as she seemed? Vicky
wondered. Or did she use her eccentric manner as a
cover for... For what? Vicky mocked her suspicions.
Sophie was simply a very nice old lady with odd taste
in costume jewelry, who didn't view reality quite the
same way the rest of the world did. And, considering
her background, that was hardly surprising. From what
Vicky had learned, the Thayer family had never lived
life as the rest of the world did.

The ormolu clock on the Adams mantel gave a sub-
dued chime, and James hurriedly set down his teacup
and got to his feet. Pushing back the sleeve of his gray
tweed jacket, he double-checked the time on his thin,
gold watch.

Vicky stared at him, rather taken aback by his eagerness. When he'd said that he saw the children every
day at four, she'd assumed that his interest in them was
more proprietary than loving. But now she wasn't so
sure.

Surreptitiously, Vicky studied his face. He looked...
hungry was the closest word she could come up with.
As if he were in a hurry to get to the nursery.

But if he really felt that way, why did he limit himself to a daily visit at four o'clock? Why not see them
more often? Nanny might be able to brush off her and
Sophie, but James Thayer wouldn't brush that easily.

Vicky knew that from personal experience. This whole situation didn't add up, and it made her very uneasy.

"Off to see the twins, dear?" Aunt Sophie gave him a loving smile. "Give them a hug from me."

"I'm going to show them to Ms. Lascoe," James said.

"Well, of course you are, dear," Aunt Sophie said.

James shot his aunt a sharp glance, wondering if her words contained a hidden meaning.

Aunt Sophie gave James a guileless look that he instinctively mistrusted. She might seem vague and fluttery, and she might have a tendency to go off on what seemed like totally unrelated tangents, but, for all that, she was quite intelligent. To say nothing of intuitive. He most emphatically didn't want her to find out just who Ms. Lascoe represented and what her coming might mean to their small family. Aunt Sophie was too old to be worried with the situation.

"Since she's a relative we ought to call her Vicky and be done with it," Sophie decreed.

If only it were that simple, James thought, having the feeling that he would never be "done with" Vicky. That nothing he could do or say would make her go away and leave him and his children alone. But Ms. Lascoe wasn't the real problem, he reminded himself. Her client was. It was Mrs. Zane Sutton and her determination to embrace motherhood that was causing all the problems. But perhaps Mrs. Sutton's impulse wouldn't last. Maybe once the novelty of the situation wore off and she discovered that babies could be a lot of trouble, she might rethink her position. The possibility cheered him slightly.

"If you'd come with me, Ms. Lascoe—"

"I told you, we're going to call her Vicky," Sophie corrected.

"Vicky," James repeated to humor his aunt, although his gut instinct told him that anything that deepened the tenuous bond between him and Ms. Lascoe was a very bad idea.

"And you are to call him James," Sophie instructed Vicky.

Vicky barely noticed the order. Her mind was totally focused on the thought that she was about to meet her children. Finally.

"Well, off you go then, m'boy," Sophie said. "The wicked witch doesn't let you see enough of the little sprigs as it is. You don't want to waste a minute of your precious visiting hour."

"Aunt Sophie, you promised," James began.

"And I kept my word. She ain't here to hear me tell the truth, is she? Now run along, boy.

Yes, run along, Vicky mentally urged him.

To her relief, James merely shook his head at his aunt's plain speaking and started out the door.

Vicky hurried after him.

Once they had reached the second floor and Sophie couldn't overhear them, Vicky decided to ask a few questions while she had the chance.

"Why doesn't Sophie like the nanny?"

"Perhaps it's a case of Dr. Fell?"

"What?"

"The old nursery rhyme. 'I do not like thee, Dr. Fell. Exactly why I cannot tell. But this I know full well, I do not like thee, Dr. Fell,'" he quoted.

Vicky wanted to tell him that, while she couldn't be sure of his great-aunt's reasons, she knew exactly why she didn't like Nanny. Because the woman was a domestic tyrant.

Two flights of stairs and three corridors later, they finally reached the white painted door that Vicky had visited earlier.

"You are not to say anything to Nanny about why you're really here," he ordered.

"You're starting to repeat yourself," Vicky snapped, her nerves stretched thin with longing. It didn't seem either fair or just that her access to her own children should be under the control of this autocratic man.

Vicky watched James's eyes widen and wondered why. Because of what she'd said? Did people normally say "yes and amen" to his every utterance? Maybe.

Her thoughts scattered into irretrievable fragments when James reached past her and knocked on the nursery door. It opened immediately.

Her breath caught in her throat, and her heart began to beat in slow, heavy strokes that threatened to deafen her. Her legs felt shaky as if they couldn't support the immensity of feeling that was flooding her.

Vicky could hear James saying something, but the words echoed meaninglessly in her ears. The only things that had any reality for her were the two small babies lying in a playpen beneath the large window.

As if their shared relationship was a magnet that drew her, Vicky walked toward them, her steps stiff with the emotions she was holding inside. They were perfect, she thought in wonder. Absolutely beautiful, with their bright blue eyes and the adorable wisps of pale yellow curls that framed their little faces.

Vicky leaned over the edge of the playpen and gazed down at them with a mixture of awe, love and pride.

To think that she was partially responsible for two such perfect human beings.

She gulped back tears when Edmond waved one chubby fist at her as if he recognized her and was saying hello. Not only beautiful but smart, she decided with a surge of maternal pride.

James frowned uncertainly as he watched the revealing emotions that illuminated Vicky's face. The naked emotion mirrored there confused him. Why was she so overwhelmed by the sight of the twins? Did she get this emotionally involved with all her cases? If so, she wasn't going to last long in law. She'd be emotionally burned out in a few years. But in the meantime her obvious identification with the twins' bio-mother's custody fight was going to make their negations that much harder.

Damn! he thought in frustration. This whole situation was becoming more complicated by the minute.

Vicky Lascoe's feelings didn't matter, he told himself. He couldn't let himself worry about her. He had to concentrate on what was best for his children. And what was best for them was to live in a stable environment. Not to be shuffled back and forth between two parents so that they never felt truly at home with either.

Edmond made one of his intriguing noises, and James watched as Vicky surreptitiously wiped a tear away from the corner of her eye.

Impelled by an impulse he didn't quite understand, James leaned down and picked up Edmond so that Vicky could see him better.

Her response wasn't what he expected. Instead of concentrating on Edmond, she immediately picked up the much quieter Mary Rose.

James held his breath, waiting for his daughter's usual response to strangers: an outraged stare followed by a shriek that would have given Jack the Ripper second thoughts about his chosen vocation. To his surprise, it didn't happen. Mary Rose looked up at Vicky as if considering the situation, and then gifted Vicky with one of her rare smiles.

James was honestly horrified at the flash of jealousy that shot through him. Surely he wasn't so petty that he resented his daughter smiling at Vicky, he thought in confusion.

"Hello, angel." Vicky dropped a light kiss on Mary Rose's small head.

"Allow me, sir." The poignant moment was shattered by the hovering nanny. "You aren't supporting Edmond properly."

Scooping Edmond out of his father's arms, Nanny carefully set him back in the playpen.

To Vicky's surprise, James's only response to the woman's dictatorial manner was a muttered "Sorry."

What was going on here? Vicky wondered. James certainly hadn't had any trouble telling her what he wanted. So why was he letting this martinet masquerading as a nanny dictate to him? It didn't make any sense. Unless...

Did he allow it because he didn't really care? Could her first assessment have been right after all? Did he not see the children as people in their own right with emotional as well as physical needs to be meet? Maybe to him the children simply fulfilled a function—that of being his heirs? Could that be why he was so determined to have control of them? Not because he loved them but because he wanted to control the child who would one day inherit all this historical magnificence?

The thought chilled her, and she hugged Mary Rose closer as if trying to protect her daughter from the cold-blooded idea. If it were true, then where did Mary Rose fit into his plans? Edmond would inherit the estate, but what about Mary Rose?

"You are holding Mary Rose too tightly." Nanny delivered the opinion as if she couldn't possibly be wrong.

"Mary Rose doesn't seem to mind." Vicky forced an even tone.

"Mary Rose is a baby," Nanny stated the obvious.

"Unarguable and also apropos of nothing," Vicky countered. "Babies are very sturdy creatures."

"These are Mr. Thayer's children!" Nanny seemed outraged at having the twins lumped in with babies in general.

"Is there something wrong with him that he makes bad babies?" Vicky snapped, annoyed at the woman's interference.

"Madam!" Nanny sputtered. "You are upsetting the children."

Vicky looked down at Mary Rose, who was contentedly blowing bubbles, and then back at Nanny's red face.

"Nonsense," Vicky said. "I'm upsetting you, not the children. What I haven't quite figured out is why."

James swallowed the urge to cheer Vicky on, reminding himself that the children needed Nanny. Not only did she come highly recommended, but the twins had thrived in her care. When he remembered what they had looked like when he'd finally been able to bring them home from the neonatal ward where they'd spent the first precarious two weeks of their lives...

Nanny might be a bit abrasive and opinionated, but her methods worked.

"You'll be wanting to feed them their dinner, Nanny," James said, trying to soothe matters over. "So we'll leave you to it."

Nanny held out her hands for Mary Rose, and Vicky had to force herself to give her the baby. She wanted to keep her daughter. To take her and Edmond and walk out of this place. To find a spot where sanity reigned. Where parents weren't kept from their children.

James saw the disappointment in Vicky's eyes, and his feeling of guilt intensified. He wasn't siding with Nanny over Vicky. He was doing what was necessary to ensure the continued well-being of his children.

Telling herself that this was simply the first scrimmage in the battle for custody of the twins, Vicky dropped a last kiss on Mary Rose's downy curls and reluctantly handed her to Nanny. Then she leaned over the playpen and rubbed her fingertips over Edmond's soft cheek before she turned to go.

She'd be back, she vowed. No matter what, she'd be back to rescue her children from this overbearing martinet.

Chapter Three

The insistent shrilling of the alarm bludgeoned its way into Vicki's troubled sleep, demanding her attention. Blindly she groped for the sadistic implement, but her fingers encountered only air where her bedside table should have been.

Confused, she prized open eyelids that felt glued together and found herself staring at the faded tapestry bed hangings that decorated her four-poster bed.

Four-poster bed? Where... Vicky jerked upright as memory came flooding back, washing away her confusion. She wasn't home in Philadelphia. She was in Merry Olde England staying in as stately a house as they came.

Jumping out of bed, she sprinted to the dresser where she'd put her travel alarm last night under the theory that having to get out of bed to turn it off would ensure that she stayed awake. She jammed the button on the alarm and breathed a sigh of relief as she was once again enveloped in blessed silence.

She stared out one of the room's three large windows at the early-morning sunshine and tried to think. If England was five hours ahead of Philadelphia time, and it was seven here, then her body thought it was...two a.m.? She wasn't quite sure about the time, but there was one thing she was sure of. She had no intention of adjusting to the time change gradually. She had too much to do. Beginning with getting to know her children.

Vicky wrapped her arms around herself in delight at the very thought of Edmond and Mary Rose. Even if she did say so herself, they were the most gorgeous children she'd ever seen. And smart, too. She smiled proudly as she remembered how intelligently Mary Rose had studied her. Exactly as if she had understood that Vicky was her mother.

Maybe she had, Vicky thought. Maybe that old saying about blood recognizing blood was really true.

But the twins also had James Thayer's blood in them. The disquieting thought intruded on her happy memories. And James Thayer was the major stumbling block to her goal of sharing in her children's lives.

But he wasn't a permanent one, she encouraged herself. He couldn't shut her out of their children's lives. She had a valid claim, as their mother, that no court would deny. She just prayed it didn't come to that. A court battle was the last resort. The absolute last resort. Not only would it inflict bitter wounds that might never heal, but the media circus that was bound to follow would dog the twins their entire lives.

No, it would be far better for everyone concerned if she and James could reach an agreement privately. Vicky sighed. Unfortunately, James Thayer was clearly a man who was used to dictating terms, not negotiating them.

Well, there was a first time for everything. He'd soon find that she wouldn't be influenced, intimidated or bought off. And when that happened, he'd have no choice left but to deal with her. And she could hurry the process along by telling him that she wasn't a representative of the twin's mother. She *was* their mother.

Vicky shivered as the memory of his implacable features filled her mind. And then again, maybe telling him the truth wouldn't help the situation. Maybe he'd try to use her impersonation as an excuse to stall. Maybe he'd order her out of the house.

Not that that strategy would work for very long. She wasn't ever going to disappear from her children's lives, and the sooner James Thayer found out that he didn't have a monopoly on determination, the quicker they could reach an agreement.

Vicky scooped up the beige twill skirt and emerald-green linen blouse she'd set out last night and stumbled toward the bathroom, hoping that a shower would make her feel a little more alert.

To her relief, it did. By the time she was dressed, she was beginning to feel almost human. She quickly combed her hair, leaving it free to brush her shoulders, added a coating of pink lipstick to her wide mouth and then stepped back to study her reflection in the mirror.

Neat, but not gaudy, she remembered her grandmother's criteria for how a woman should look, then paused, wondering what kind of criteria James had. Certainly not neat, she thought. More likely, sophisticated teamed with drop-dead gorgeous.

The thought unexpectedly depressed her, but only because she didn't want her children to learn to judge a person by their looks, she told herself.

As she left her room, Vicky briefly considered going to the nursery first to see the twins, but decided against it. She wasn't sure how to get there and she didn't want to be discovered wandering around the corridors on her first morning here.

James ought to provide his visitors with a map of the house, she thought wryly. Either that or give them a compass.

She found her way back to the main hall where she met Beech. A quick question elicited the information that coffee could be had in the breakfast room. Vicky turned down his offer of an escort and hurried toward the promised restorative.

While she was fortifying her system with a hefty dose of caffeine, she'd figure out how to word her confession about her real identity, she decided. Then she'd go find the master of the house and get it over with.

Vicky walked through the third archway on her left as Beech had instructed and came to a precipitous halt when she discovered that the room already had an occupant. James Thayer was sitting at a round table, the remains of his breakfast in front of him, reading a newspaper.

The bright morning sunlight pouring through the window's small panes of leaded glass fragmented into a rainbow of individual colors that clung to him, gilding his lean face with a bluish-purple tint that made her think of archangels.

James looked up, and Vicky's impression of otherworldliness was irrevocably lost beneath the direct impact of his eyes. They seemed to burn into her, judging her and finding her wanting.

Get a grip, woman, Vicky ordered herself. She was letting this place get to her. James Thayer was only a man. He could only see the image she projected. He had no way of knowing what she was thinking. He might have more of the world's goods than anyone she'd ever met, but that didn't change the fact that he was just a man.

Of their own accord, her eyes slipped over the brown tweed jacket he was wearing, measuring the breadth of his shoulders. He certainly was a man. And that was part of the trouble, she conceded. She kept seeing him as an attractive man, and she couldn't figure out why.

Particularly given the fact that she didn't like forceful men. James Thayer had to rank as the most forceful man she'd ever run across. He made her first husband's attempts at domination look like child's play.

What was that old expression, "What's bred in the bone comes out in the blood"? That described James perfectly. He was the end result of centuries of dominant males, and it showed. It most definitely showed.

You were the top student in your assertiveness workshop, she reminded herself, to bolster her sinking spirits. You were voted most likely to not get stomped on again by your fellow students. But then, she doubted if any of her fellow students had ever run across anyone like James Thayer. She had the distinct feeling he would have proved a challenge for the workshop's teacher.

"Good morning." James got to his feet with an instinctive bow that appealed to her. "I didn't expect to see you at this hour."

"It's seven-thirty," Vicky said.

"True." James studied her as she slipped into the chair across from him.

Did she normally come down for breakfast? he wondered. Or was this something she was doing for his benefit. But why would she bother? She could talk to him any time she wanted. She didn't have to get up early to do it. With the question of his children's future security at stake, he had no intention of avoiding her.

He wanted to use every opportunity to make her see just how important it was for her to convince Mrs. Sutton to leave the children in his sole care where they were clearly thriving.

Vicky Lascoe could be a powerful ally if he could just get her to put the children's interest above her client's selfish desire to play mother to two children she'd never even meet.

"Do you prefer to eat alone?" Vicky asked with a quick glance at the newspaper and the pile of letters sitting beside his empty plate. She was torn between wanting him to say yes so she could escape his disturbing presence and wanting him to ask her to stay. Such dithering wasn't like her and, if she hadn't had so much else to worry about, it would have bothered her. As it was, she barely gave it a thought.

"It isn't a question of my preference," James said. "Aunt Sophie doesn't leave her room until after ten."

"I see," Vicky murmured, wondering what his ex-wife had preferred. Had Romayne also slept late instead of breakfasting with her husband? Or maybe they had breakfasted in their room together? The thought sent an uncomfortable flash of emotion through Vicky that made her uneasy.

"Daniel, would you bring Ms. Lascoe some breakfast?"

Vicky turned to find a middle-aged man wearing a white jacket standing behind her.

"Certainly, sir," Daniel said. "What would you like Ms. Lascoe?"

"Just coffee, please." Vicky said.

"Coffee does not constitute breakfast," James said. "Do you want cereal or eggs?"

Vicky wanted to tell him that she had already ordered what she'd wanted. Coffee. Which was all her poor, confused stomach felt up to coping with at the moment, but she didn't want to make a scene under Daniel's curious gaze. Nor did she want to start the day fighting with James. No doubt hostilities would break out with a vengeance once he found out who she really was, but for now she might as well try for peace.

"An egg will be fine," she said.

"Won't be a minute," Daniel said. "In the meantime I'll give you a nice hot cup of coffee." He poured a steaming cup out of the ornate silver pot sitting on the mahogany sideboard and placed it on the table in front of her.

"Thank you," Vicky murmured to his retreating back and gratefully reached for the dark, reviving liquid.

James watched her add sugar and cream, his eyes lingering on the paleness of her fair skin and the dark smudges beneath her eyes. She looked exhausted. As if she hadn't had any sleep at all. Or...

"When did you arrive in England?" James asked.

"Yesterday morning," Vicky said, taking a deep swallow of the excellent coffee.

"And came right here?"

"Of course I came right here. I'm only in England to see the twins and this is where they are."

"So your body thinks it's still the middle of the night," he concluded. "You should have spent a couple of days in London adjusting to the time difference."

"Why? The time there is the same as it is here," Vicky said tartly.

"Take a nap this afternoon," he ordered.

"I'll take your suggestion under advisement," she murmured, trying out the workshop technique of dealing with arbitrary orders by acknowledging them. "But don't feel that you have to entertain me. Feel free to read your paper."

"I've already finished," James said.

"Then read your letters," Vicky said, finding it disconcerting to have his entire attention focused on her. It made her feel…uneasy, she finally decided.

"You certainly have enough letters," she encouraged.

"They're just business," James said, dismissing them.

Business? Vicky was caught off guard by his comment. The real Ms. Lascoe had told her that James had inherited a great deal of wealth along with this estate, an even bigger one in the Scottish Highlands and a townhouse in London in the Mayfair district. She'd simply assumed that he lived on his income and spent his days enjoying himself.

Although her assumption had been based on nothing more factual than a newspaper article she'd once read in the more lurid press about how the English aristocracy spent its time. But this particular aristocrat didn't seem to lend himself to easy categorization. He was turning out to be a far more complex personality than she'd expected.

Daniel's return interrupted her thoughts. He set a very thin, cream-colored plate containing two eggs and a couple of pieces of fried bread in front of her.

"Cook says if you want anything else to be sure to let her know," Daniel said as he placed a setting of ornately carved silverware on the table beside the plate.

"This is fine," Vicky said. "Please thank the cook for her efforts."

"I will, ma'am. Will there be anything else, sir?"

"No, that'll be all, Daniel."

Vicky studied the fried eggs with a jaundiced eye.

Hadn't they heard about cholesterol on this side of the Atlantic?

Picking up the heavy silver folk, Vicky cautiously ate a little of the white of the eggs. She loathed runny yolks.

To her relief, James started to read his mail instead of watching her eat.

She was carefully spreading lime marmalade on her fried bread when James muttered, "Damned idiots!"

She glanced across the table to find him glaring at a seemingly innocuous sheet of paper.

He grabbed a gold pen off the table, scribbled something in the margin of the letter and then flung the sheet to one side as if it were harboring something contagious.

"What exactly do you do?" Vicky asked. Not that she was curious on her own behalf, she assured herself. It was just that she needed to know what made James Thayer tick if she was ever to be successful at convincing him to share custody of their children with her.

"I'm a venture capitalist."

"A venture capitalist?" Vicky repeated, trying to fit a job description to the title. She couldn't.

"I match people with ideas to people with money to invest," he responded to her blank look. "You'd undoubtedly find it boring."

"Do you have a particular reason for your opinion or is it simply the same knee-jerk, patronizing response you'd give any woman who asked about your business?" she retorted.

"I was not being patronizing," he defended himself. "It's just that the women I've known have not found business to be of any interest."

The women? Vicky examined his response. How many women was he referring to? Someone with

James's money and looks would have his pick of
women, and when you added his aristocratic background... He probably had to beat them off with a
stick.

The thought disturbed her, but only because a steady
stream of women through James's life would be very
upsetting for the twins, she told herself. He was a father
now. A man with family responsibilities. If he wasn't
willing to put his social life on hold while the twins
were little, he should let her have custody because she
was willing to do it. In fact, she had no desire to ever
become emotionally involved with a man on any mean-
ingful level again. Once had been more than enough.

"Are you interested in business?" he asked.

"No, I find it boring." Vicky's sudden grin sent a
surge of heat through him. He looked closer at the soft
lips forming the smile. They looked warm and infinitely inviting.

Don't go there, James warned himself. Vicky Lascoe
was off-limits. At the moment, her loyalty was to Mrs.
Sutton. Getting emotionally involved with her would
only complicate a situation that was already unbeliev-
ably complicated.

"What do you base *your* opinion on?" James made
a monumental effort to focus on her words and not the
lips uttering them.

"On two years of trying to run my father's whole-
sale plumbing-supply business." The truth slipped out
before she remembered that she was supposed to be
Ms. Lascoe.

Vicky held her breath in sudden fear that James
might know that it was Mrs. Sutton's father who had
been in plumbing and not Ms. Lascoe's.

She felt almost limp with relief when his expression

didn't change. Apparently, he hadn't gone into her background in any depth. Not that he'd had much time.

Plumbing supplies? James studied her delicate features, trying to imagine her selling plumbing supplies of all things. His imagination wasn't equal to the task.

"What made you choose the law as a profession?" he asked, curious as to how her mind worked.

"The law?" Vicky repeated slowly as she frantically scrambled to remember what she knew about the law. She drew an absolute blank. As far as she was concerned, the law was a closed book that she'd never had the slightest desire to open.

Vicky stared down at the fast-congealing eggs on her plate and tried to decide if this was the time to confess. To admit who she really was and hope that he wouldn't kick her out before she even had a chance to get to see her children again.

The skin on her arms tightened in pleasurable memory as she remembered the soft, sweet weight of Mary Rose filling them. She wanted to hold her again. To pick up Edmond and kiss his dear little head. To snuggle them close and simply revel in the fact that they were hers. Her children.

She stole a quick glance at James, and her gaze collided with his strong chin. An icy shiver slithered down her spine. Not yet, she decided. Not until she'd had a chance to plan the wording of her confession so he'd understand. And not until she'd had a chance to see the twins again. She'd tell him tonight. That way she would at least have had today with Edmond and Mary Rose.

In the meantime, she needed to get the conversation off the subject of law and onto something where she could hold up her end of the conversation.

"My father and grandfather were lawyers, and I just

kind of drifted into it," Vicky repeated what the real
Ms. Lascoe had told her. "If I had to do it again, I
think I'd be a Latin professor."

"Latin?" he repeated aloud, wondering if he had
misunderstood her.

"Yes, the classical variety. I have no interest in the
way the language was bastardized in the Middle Ages.
The Church has a lot to answer for!" Vicky scowled,
and her outraged expression intrigued him. He'd never
known a woman to get upset with the language of the
Medieval church. Or a man, either, for that matter.

"Classical Latin is a rather unusual interest," he
probed.

"By whose standards?" Vicky asked. "Certainly
not mine."

"I wasn't making a value judgment," he said. "I
was merely a little taken aback. Somehow, an interest
in selling plumbing supplies and reading classical Latin
don't seem compatible."

"But I wasn't interested in plumbing. That was the
problem." Vicki's features momentarily took on a
bleakness that James found chilling. He wanted to take
her in his arms and tell her that it didn't matter. Not
that he had the slightest idea what had caused her expression. Nor did he really think she needed protecting.
Every woman he had ever met had been more than
capable of protecting her own interests. Except his poor
aunt Sophie, and she was the exception that proved the
rule.

"How did you develop an interest in Latin?" he
asked.

"My grandfather used to play bridge with a Jesuit."

James frowned, trying to see a connection. He
couldn't.

"What does the one have to do with the other?" he finally asked.

"Father Auggie taught Latin at the local university, and I was fascinated by the Latin books he used to carry around, so he taught me, too."

"How old were you?"

"In second grade when he started the Latin. He added classical Greek the following year because he wanted me to be well-rounded." A tender smile curved her lips at the halcyon memory of those long-ago, uncomplicated days when the world had seemed so bright and shining, so filled with infinite possibilities. But it wasn't true; her smile dimmed as she remembered how that future had turned into a present filled with the pain of loss and the regret of wrong choices. Like Zane. Her expression grew bleak.

James watched the animation bleed from her face with an almost personal sense of loss. He wanted to distract her from whatever unhappy thoughts gripped her.

"If you like Latin and..." He gestured toward her plate.

Vicky's eyes automatically followed the gesture he made with one well-shaped hand. In just such a forceful manner might a Roman emperor have spared the life of a gladiator. Her eyes met his, and she shivered at his alert expression. Or condemned him to death, she reminded herself.

"If you're through playing with your breakfast?"

"Yes." Vicky made no attempt to justify her lack of appetite. Not when she hadn't wanted the eggs in the first place.

"Then I'd like to show you the library. There are several Latin books in it that you might find interesting."

"Please." Vicky hurriedly got to her feet, wanting to take advantage of his offer before he changed his mind. She wasn't sure if his invitation qualified as a friendly gesture or if he was simply trying to find something to keep her busy. Either way, she had no intention of turning him down. She was curious as to what might be in the library. Especially considering some of the things she'd already seen in his house.

James dropped his heavy, damask napkin on the table and got to his feet.

"The main library is on the other side of the Great Hall," he said as he lead the way.

"How many years did it take you to find your way around this place without getting lost?" Vicky envied him the sureness with which he moved.

"Lost?" He glanced at her. "The house isn't that big."

"Ha! Not only is it that big, but it's built like a rabbit warren."

"That's because it's old. The original portion was part of a monastery Peregrine Thayer was given after the Reformation.

"He extensively rebuilt around the original core. And various Thayers since have added on, usually with no thought to what the overall effect would be," he added dryly.

Vicky was silent as she tried to imagine what it would be like to belong to a family that lived in a house given as a royal gift over five hundred years ago. Her own family had migrated to America from Italy after World War I to escape the grinding poverty of their subsistence farm.

The disparity between her and James's backgrounds worried her. What would the twins think when they were old enough to compare their father's illustrious family with their mother's hardworking, middle-class one?

That was all the more reason why she had to play a pivotal role in their upbringing, she told herself. She couldn't allow them to be raised as snobs. She needed to make them understand from an early age that it wasn't what your ancestors had done that mattered. What mattered was what you did with your own life.

James paused in front of a set of ornately carved double doors and pushed one open. At his gesture she went inside, coming to a precipitous stop just inside the doorway.

"Good heavens," Vicky murmured with disbelieving awe as she stared around the huge room. It must have been sixty feet long and about thirty feet wide. The wall to her right was punctuated by a series of eight-foot windows that let in the sunlight and gave the room's occupants a soothing view of the back gardens. Ceiling-to-floor shelves lined every available bit of wall space.

"What a fantastic room," she breathed reverently.

"I'm rather fond of it." James was gratified by her obvious approval. "The Latin texts I wanted to show you are over here."

He started toward the opposite end of the room, and Vicky trailed along behind him, trying to read titles as she went. She came to a sudden stop when her attention was caught by three small prints about one-foot-by-two-feet that were hanging between two windows.

She peered closer. They were maps. Either very old maps or extremely good facsimiles.

"James, what are these?"

"Maps." He answered her question literally, surprised at her interest. He'd personally hung those prints there over twenty-five years ago, and she was the first woman who had ever even noticed them, let alone commented on them.

"I can see that!" she said impatiently. "But what kind of maps and from where?"

"They're reputed to be copies of the maps of Peri Reese and they date from the Medieval period that you think so little of."

"Where did you get them?"

"From a drawer in the munitions room. I discovered them when I was still at Eton and, since my parents weren't here to object, I had them framed and hung them in here."

"I see," Vicky muttered, seeing nothing of the sort. She had no idea why his parents wouldn't have been here. Especially since it sounded as if this was where James had spent his childhood. What kind of childhood would it have been without parents around? She couldn't begin to imagine.

Her own parents' presence had been a loving constant in her life. If she had found some old maps and had wanted to frame them, her parents would have helped her mat them, frame them and hang them on the wall. Then they would have proudly taken pictures of her standing in front of her handiwork. And all James remembered was that his parents hadn't been there to object. Was that the kind of parenting he intended to use with her children? The thought chilled her.

Vicky stole a quick glance at James to find him staring at the maps with a withdrawn expression that discouraged further questions. He looked as if he were remembering something unpleasant or painful. Surely the maps hadn't caused it. Not when he'd been full of enthusiasm just a moment before. So what had prompted his withdrawal? Her question? Had it reminded him of his childhood?

Vicky stifled a sigh. She didn't know. And she couldn't even make an intelligent guess, because she knew virtually nothing about James Thayer. All she knew were the relatively unimportant things which anyone reading *Burke's Peerage* could find out.

No, she corrected herself, she knew two other things. She knew he was the father of her children and he had an interest in old maps.

"The books I wanted to show you are up here."

He pulled a library ladder over and climbed up it to reach a book on the shelf just above his head.

Vicky watched as his suit jacket pulled upward, giving her a clear view of his long legs topped by flat hips. Nervously, she ran her tongue over her lower lip as she studied the way the muscles in his thighs bunched as he stretched a bit more. He had the most masculine-looking body she'd ever seen.

Instinctively she inched closer to him. Close enough to become aware of the woodsy scent of the cologne he was wearing. She took a deep breath, drawing the intoxicating aroma deeper into her lungs.

She discovered that it wasn't enough. She wanted more. She wanted to nuzzle her face against his neck. She wanted to tease open the buttons on his crisp white shirt and push her fingers into the opening. She wanted to rub her cheek over his—

A sharp rap on the door cut into her fantasies, and she jumped back, praying no hint of what she'd been feeling was visible on her face. It was bad enough that she was consumed with sexual curiosity about James Thayer. It would be mortifying if anyone else noticed.

James turned from his perusal of the shelves and called, "Come in."

The door opened to reveal Beech.

"Mr. Thayer, Herr Murchin is on the phone. He said he has the figures you asked for yesterday."

"Thank you, Beech. I'll take it in the study."

So she couldn't overhear his conversation? Vicky wondered. If that was his motivation, he could save himself the trouble. She had no leanings toward industrial spying.

"Feel free to look over the library," James said perfunctorily, and then hurried after Beech.

"Thank you," Vicky muttered in frustration to the empty library. Much as she loved books and wanted to explore this unexpected treasure trove, she wanted to see her children far more.

Patience, she counseled herself. This was only a very minor setback. When James came back from his phone call, she'd demand that he allow her to see the children. Right then. Not at the witching hour of four. And she wouldn't take no for an answer.

Chapter Four

Vicky reread the same line of Latin text for the fourth time with no more understanding than she had gotten the previous three times. Sighing, she carefully closed the fragile volume and set it on the ormolu table beside the wing chair she was sitting in.

As enthralling as she would have normally found the book, it couldn't hold her attention. She simply didn't care about Latin right now. Now all she cared about was seeing her children.

Vicky glared at the heavy library doors in frustration. It was becoming increasingly clear to her that James wasn't going to come back. If she wanted to get permission from him to see her children, she was going to have to go and find him.

Vicky pressed her lips together in anger. She shouldn't have to ask his permission. Even if he did think she was simply the twins' mother's lawyer, she still had a right to see them. A right he had acknowledged by agreeing to let her assess their development.

Something she could hardly do without spending time with them. James had to know that. He wasn't dumb. Far from it. She shivered as she remembered the intelligence shimmering in his dark eyes.

So why was he stalling? What did he hope to gain at this point? Unfortunately, she didn't know. There was so much about this whole situation that she didn't know, and she wasn't even sure how to go about finding out. Simply asking wasn't going to work. He'd just deny it as he had the last time.

Restlessly, Vicky got to her feet, wandered over to one of the long windows and looked out. Maybe she could...

Her tentative plans were suspended as she saw a woman in a navy-blue uniform pushing an oversize pram across the lawn.

Instinctively, Vicky leaned forward to see better. It was the twins and Attila the Nanny! Outside, where there were no doors for the blasted woman to shut in her face.

Vicky's gaze swept the empty lawn. No James, either, to take Nanny's side against her. This was her chance.

Vicky's heart began to thump with excitement. Not waiting to find a door to the outside, she simply yanked up the window, climbed over the low sill, stepped onto the terrace, ran the length of the house and hurried toward them.

She had almost reached the twins when Nanny looked up and saw her. Vicky barely noticed the irritated expression that crossed Nanny's face in her eagerness to reach her children.

However, it was impossible not to notice when

Nanny suddenly swung the pram around, putting herself between Vicky and her children.

"I want to play with Edmond and Mary Rose." Vicky forced the level words out. Antagonizing the blasted woman would simply slow things down. Maybe she could make friends with her.

Vicky stared into Nanny's implacable brown eyes. And then again, maybe she couldn't. Mary Poppins this lady wasn't.

"Play!" Nanny repeated incredulously.

"What part of the concept don't you understand?" Vicky's tenuous composure began to crack slightly, allowing her frustration to seep out.

"It is time for their airing," Nanny stated. "They don't play now."

"Fine, I'll walk them." Vicky wasn't about to give up. Not this close to her children.

"*I* give them their airing," Nanny announced. "You are disturbing them."

Vicky looked over Nanny's shoulder at her children. Edmond was energetically chewing on his fist, and Mary Rose was watching her with an intensity that convinced Vicky the baby knew who she was.

"They aren't the least bit upset," Vicky said.

"And I intend to keep them that way." Nanny shoved the pram forward, leaving Vicky behind.

Vicky watched Nanny head back to the house in impotent anger. She wanted to run after her, grab the carriage handle and physically wrest it away from the blasted woman. The very strength of the urge gave her pause. Closing her eyes, she took a deep breath and then took a second when the first wasn't enough to dissipate the fury ripping through her.

She absolutely could not fight Nanny for the carriage, she told herself. It would frighten the children. And even if it didn't, physically confronting Nanny would have repercussions. Nanny wasn't the type to take defeat in silence. She'd undoubtedly run to James with a wildly exaggerated tale of assault, and he'd probably use Nanny's lies as an excuse to get rid of her.

Besides, Nanny wasn't the real problem, Vicky reminded herself. The real problem was James's refusal to tell the woman that Vicky was to be given access to the twins, when and as often as she wanted it.

And since James was the major stumbling block to her getting to see the twins, the sooner she tackled him the better. Dread dried her mouth at the thought of the argument that was bound to ensue when she stopped asking for permission to see the twins and started demanding it.

She could handle James Thayer. Vicky firmly quashed her doubts. All she had to do was to remember the techniques she'd learned in her assertiveness training workshop.

It took Vicky ten minutes to locate Beech and find out that James was in his study. She turned down the butler's offer to announce her under the theory that this kind of situation definitely called for a surprise attack.

A perfunctory knock on the study door was her only concession to the social conventions. Without waiting for an answer, she shoved open the door and marched inside.

She instantly located James. He was seated behind a huge mahogany desk writing on a legal-size notepad.

She watched as he glanced up, and his eyes narrowed slightly at the sight of her. Annoyed that she had invaded his sanctuary? she wondered nervously.

"May I help you?" he asked.

"You haven't been very helpful to date," she launched her offensive. "In fact, you've been downright obstructive. Just how dumb do you think I am?

"No, strike that last question," she hurriedly said as his eyebrows rose in what she was sure was mock surprise. "What you think of me is irrelevant."

If only it were, James thought wryly. Unfortunately, he was afraid that his unexpected and totally irrational fascination with Vicky Lascoe was coloring his perception of the whole situation.

"Your plan isn't going to work."

James spent a moment studying her determined expression and then asked, "Which plan is that?"

"Telling Nanny not to let me see the twins, of course! I am here to assess the children, and I can't do that if I can't interact with them."

"I didn't tell Nanny not to let you see them." Hell, he'd never told Nanny anything. She was the one who told him.

"I don't believe you!" Vicky spurted out. "The woman works for you. She gets her instructions from you."

"Wrong, she gets her salary from me. She doesn't get instructions from me. I don't know anything about babies."

"And at the rate you're going, they're going to grow up with you still not knowing anything about them. If you don't care enough to learn what the babies need and want, then let their mother have custody of them. She's willing to put in the effort to find out."

James scowled at her, and Vicky tightened the muscles in her legs, which were showing a tendency to quiver. She had to stand her ground. Giving in didn't solve problems. She reminded herself of the hard-learned lesson from her first marriage. All giving in did was postpone the reckoning. And when the bill finally did come due, it came with a lot of added interest.

"Babies have very specialized needs. And one of those needs is adherence to a strict schedule." James quoted Nanny.

"Babies need lots of love, along with nutritious food and a safe environment. Nanny might be providing the last two," Vicky conceded, "but don't try to tell me that that woman has even a passing acquaintance with love!"

"Simply because she doesn't act besotted doesn't mean that she isn't…isn't…fond of them," James finally said.

"Fond!" Vicky was outraged. "My—" she caught herself in time "—*client's* children are supposed to make due with 'fond' when they have a mother prepared to love them?"

"They aren't making due with 'fond'!" James snapped, but Vicky never even noticed his anger, her own sense of outrage was too great. "I love them."

"Sure, between four and five every day."

"Nanny says…"

"Nanny be damned!"

James looked into Vicky's face, his eyes lingering on the hectic flush burning across the translucent skin of her cheekbones. She looked angry and determined and…and uncomfortable, he realized. As if this confrontation were not something that she welcomed. As if she were as ill at ease with this argument as he was. But that didn't make any sense. She was the one who'd come in here and started it. Not only that, she was a lawyer, and in the States lawyers argued in court all the time. It was an integral part of their job. If someone didn't like confrontation why would they choose the law as a profession?

He frowned. There was something about this whole situation he was missing, but he couldn't quite put his finger on it. It bothered him. He didn't like things that didn't add up. Particularly when they were in his own house.

"Nanny has been very good for the children," James finally said. "However," he hurriedly added when Vicky opened her mouth, "I admit I did agree to let you have access to the twins so you could report back to your client about how well they are doing here."

"Report to their biological mother," Vicky muttered.

James ignored the correction.

"I will make it clear to Nanny that you are allowed to see Edmond and Mary Rose whenever you wish." And then I'll pray she doesn't get furious and quit over my interference with her schedule, James thought uneasily.

Vicky felt almost euphoric at his capitulation. She could hardly believe it. He had actually given in. Her hard-learned assertiveness techniques had worked.

James watched the pleasure lighting her eyes, taken aback by the depth of her reaction. She obviously took her client's interests very much to heart. How much would her sympathies for Mrs. Sutton influence her assessments of the twins? Would she be able to judge the situation with an unbiased eye? Could she be open-minded enough to see that the twins were doing well and should be left in his sole care or would she only consider what Mrs. Sutton wanted and not the best interests of the twins?

Like so much else in this whole mess, he didn't know.

"I'm going to see the twins now," Vicky said. "Right this minute." She watched him cautiously to make sure he wasn't about to do an about-face and forbid it.

"I'll come with you and explain to Nanny," James said.

He got to his feet, filled with an odd combination of emotions: worry over how Nanny might react to the news, anticipation at seeing the twins in the morning and pleasure over the excitement that brightened Vicky's face.

"Thank you," she said. She would rather have had the twins entirely to herself, but without James to run interference for her, she wasn't likely to even get inside the nursery.

Vicky hurried along beside James as they made their way to the nursery almost skipping in her eagerness to get there. She felt as if it were Christmas morning and she was on her way to see what wondrous delights Santa Claus had left her.

"How much experience have you had with children?" James question caught her off guard.

"Experience?" Vicky repeated as she considered his words. During her high school years, she'd baby-sat for the toddler who'd lived next door to her, and he had graduated as valedictorian of his class.

And while she could hardly claim that her watching him Saturday nights was responsible for his academic accomplishments, at least she hadn't done any damage to his emerging psyche.

"Do you often evaluate children in situations like

this?'' James rephrased his question when she didn't respond.

''I have never run across a situation like this in all my years of practicing law.'' Vicky quoted the real Ms. Lascoe.

All her years? James studied her. She didn't look old enough to be a real lawyer, let alone to be talking about all her years of practicing law.

''How long have you been a lawyer?'' he asked, curious about her background.

''Sometimes it seems like forever,'' Vicky hedged. She didn't know how long Ms. Lascoe had been a lawyer, but she was relatively certain that finding out when she'd been admitted to the bar would be an easy piece of information for anyone with access to a computer to find out, let alone someone with James Thayer's resources. She didn't want him finding out her real identity until she was ready to tell him, and that wouldn't be until she'd had a chance to spend some time with the twins. Seeing her children and getting to know them was far more important than putting James in possession of all the facts.

Turning the corner of the hallway and seeing the nursery door, Vicky forgot all about the ethics of lying about her identity. Forgot everything but her consuming need to see Edmond and Mary Rose.

Her step unconsciously quickened.

James sped up to keep pace with her and glanced down at her face, a little taken aback by the eagerness he saw there. She was certainly a woman who took her work very seriously.

Would she bring that same sense of urgency and passion to making love? The unexpected thought popped into his head sending a wave of heat through him. Don't go there. He hastily clamped off an image of Vicky, wearing a sheer bit of blue silk, lying in the middle of his huge antique bed smiling up at him. Vicky Lascoe was in league with the enemy—he tried to dampen his ardor with the truth.

James peered down at her. Her face was aglow with anticipation and her slender body seemed to strain toward the closed nursery door as if she could open it with nothing more than the force of her will. He found it impossible to think of her as anyone's enemy. She looked harmless.

Vicky threw an impatient glance at him as they reached the nursery door. He could see emotions seething just beneath the surface of her bright, blue eyes. No, he amended his opinion. Whatever else Vicky Lascoe was, she wasn't harmless.

Responding to her unspoken command, he knocked on the door.

It was opened a few minutes later by Amy, the maid who helped Nanny during the days.

Vicky waited for the awed-looking young woman to invite them in, and when she didn't, said, "Hi, I've come to play with the children."

"Play with the children?" Amy stared at Vicky as if she'd suggested staging a pagan sacrifice.

"Yes, play." Vicky's voice developed an edge despite her attempts to keep it neutral. What was it with everyone in this place? Why did they all find the idea of playing with babies so mind-boggling?

"May we come in?"

Amy threw a nervous glance at the silent James. "Um, I'll ask Nanny," Amy began.

"That was a rhetorical question," Vicky said.

Amy blinked as if searching her mind for a definition of *rhetorical*. Clearly, she didn't find it.

"Meaning I'm not asking permission." Vicky started forward, and Amy instinctively fell back.

There was no one in the large day nursery, so Vicky headed toward the open door in the far wall. James hurried after her, while Amy trailed along behind them as if trying to distance herself from the whole situation.

"Who was it, Amy?" Nanny's voice demanded as they entered what appeared to be a combination dining room and bedroom. There was a pair of white cribs against the far wall while near the empty fireplace stood a pair of ornately carved wooden high chairs.

Edmond sat in the one on Vicky's right while Mary Rose was in the one on her left. Seated between them was Nanny holding a bowl of something in her hand.

Nanny turned, her face tightening when she saw Vicky.

"Hi, Nanny." Vicky made an effort to be polite even though the expression on Nanny's face was anything but welcoming.

"I am feeding the twins," Nanny stated in a forbidding tone.

"Yes, well..." James began.

Vicky hastily interrupted him, afraid he was about to apologize for coming at an inconvenient time and would offer to come back later. As far as Vicky was concerned there was no such thing as an inconvenient time for a mother to see her children.

"I came to see Edmond and Mary Rose, and Mr. Thayer came along to tell you that it's all right. That I can see them any time I want. Isn't that right, James?"

Vicky gave him a look. Demand and appeal were mixed with her other less understood emotions.

"Yes, Nanny. Ms. Lascoe is to be allowed to interact with the twins whenever she wants," James stated.

"And what about their schedule?" Nanny demanded in outraged tones.

Stuff their schedule! Vicky wanted to say, but she didn't. At the moment Nanny just didn't like her, but it wouldn't take much to turn the woman into an outright enemy. And while Vicky didn't care on her own behalf, the woman did appear to have done a good job of caring for the twins. She deserved some consideration.

"I'm sure Ms. Lascoe will try not to interfere, won't you?"

James gave Vicky a hopeful look.

"I will do my best to accommodate the twins' schedule." Childishly, Vicky crossed her fingers at the lie. As far as she was concerned, loving the twins beat a strict schedule all to pieces.

"As you can see, at the moment the twins are having their lunch. Perhaps Ms. Lascoe could come back later," Nanny said. "Say about four."

Yeah, during visiting hour at the zoo, Vicky thought angrily.

"No," Vicky said, knowing she had to take a firm stand. "I'll feed them, and you can take a break."

"You?" Nanny stared at Vicky as if she'd said something obscene.

"Why is it that no one in this place seems to believe what I say?" Vicky muttered. "I said I will feed them. What is so hard to comprehend about that?"

"It takes practice to feed a baby properly," Nanny said.

"Nonsense, all it takes is common sense and patience."

Vicky determinedly held out her hand for the bowl of pale tan goo.

Nanny glanced at James, and, when help wasn't forthcoming from him, she gave the bowl to Vicky, reluctance in every line of her body.

"Why don't you go—" Vicky thought better of using the word *away* and substituted, "—rest a bit."

Nanny, with a grim expression, marched out of the room.

Vicky felt a wave of pure euphoria sweep through her. She'd done it. She'd faced down that obnoxious woman.

Sitting down in the chair Nanny had vacated, Vicky picked up the spoon filled with cereal and offered it to Edmond. He swiped at it with one pudgy hand, and Vicky hastily jerked it back.

Edmond gurgled enchantingly as if he'd just discovered a new game.

"Do they both eat that stuff out of the same bowl?" James looked askance at it.

"Since there is only one bowl and one spoon that would be my guess," Vicky said.

"Good Lord, surely the kitchen can rise to a set of bowls and their own spoons," James muttered.

"It does seem a little germy," Vicky agreed, "but then neither of them seem to have anything wrong with them."

"No, they had their six-month checkup two weeks ago and they were fine," James agreed.

"Let's try Nanny's way for the time being and see how it goes," Vicky said. She gave Mary Rose a spoonful of the stuff and the little girl obediently swallowed it and then smiled angelically. Edmond, sensing he was being upstaged, let out a howl, and Vicky hastily shoved a second spoonful into his open mouth. He grinned, dribbling a little of the concoction down his chin.

"What is that disgusting-looking pap, anyway?" James demanded as Vicky alternated spoonfuls between the twins.

"I don't know, but I hope it's water soluble," Vicky muttered as Edmond wiped some off his chin and then rubbed it into his pale blond hair.

James stuck his forefinger in the bowl and tasted the cereal. An appalled expression crossed his face.

"That is disgusting."

"It must be healthy," Vicky said dubiously. "I mean look at them. They practically radiate well-being."

Edmond chose that moment to spit his last spoonful of gruel down the front of himself.

James chuckled. "What they radiate are bad manners."

"Manners are culturally defined," Vicky said. "Why don't you clean him off while I see if Mary Rose has had all she wants?"

"Clean him off?" James repeated uncertainly, eyeing his son.

"Sure, use that washcloth," Vicky pointed to the damp cloth sitting on the table beside her.

Gingerly James picked it up and ineffectively daubed at the gruel on Edmond's face. Edmond kept twisting away, making the job impossible.

"He won't sit still," James complained.

"Allow me, Mr. Thayer," Nanny spoke from behind them, and Vicky jumped in shock. She hadn't heard the woman return.

Nanny took the cloth out of James's hand and thoroughly washed Edmond's face despite his attempts to squirm away.

Vicky wanted to grabbed the cloth out of Nanny's competent hands and hit her upside the head with it. What did it matter if James didn't do as good a job as Nanny did? What mattered was that Edmond's father was actively involving himself in his son's care. In the long run that would mean more to Edmond's development and happiness than having a perfectly clean face ever would.

But Vicky bit her tongue, reminding herself that Rome wasn't built in a day. Nor were tyrants toppled in a week. It would take time to circumvent Nanny and to convince James that he was perfectly capable of caring for his children.

"I think they've finished all they want," Vicky said.

"They each need to eat six ounces of oatmeal," Nanny stated dogmatically. "It is full of vitamins and minerals."

"It's certainly not full of taste," James muttered. "That stuff could double for library paste. Not only does it stick like glue, but no self-respecting bug would eat it."

"We are attempting to build strong bodies, sir!" Nanny's voice had an edge to it.

"Babies don't have well-developed taste buds," Vicky said soothingly, having no idea if it were true or not. She might not like Nanny and her overbearing ways, but she couldn't deny the fact that Edmond and Mary Rose were thriving in her care. At least, physically.

"And they never will, eating that gloop," James muttered under his breath.

"I will have to give the twins a bath," Nanny announced with a jaundiced look at Edmond's hair, which was now standing up in gruel-stiffened spikes. He looked for all the world like a baby biker, and Vicky was unable to entirely suppress a giggle at the sight.

Nanny's lips tightened, and Vicky considered explaining what she found humorous, then decided not to. Nanny wasn't in any mood to appreciate the humor.

"And it's time for us to see about our own lunch," James said, breaking into the lengthening silence.

"Okay." Vicky's voice sounded insincere even to her own ears. What she wanted to do was to stay and help put the twins down for their naps. To give them a cuddle and sing them a lullaby or two, but she'd gotten enough for the moment. She would come back later.

And next time Nanny wouldn't be able to shut her out.

Chapter Five

"There you are, James." Sophie glanced up from the notebook she was studying. "I was about to start lunch without you."

"I'm sorry," James said, holding the chair for Vicky to sit. "We got held up."

Vicky brushed against him as she slipped into her seat. The rough texture of his Harris tweed jacket scraping over her arm raised prickles of awareness. An awareness that raced through her veins, heating her skin as it passed. For the first time in her life she truly understood the term *hot and bothered*. And she didn't like it. Not one little bit.

It was too unsettling. Too outside her experience. And even more worrisome, it was too distracting. She couldn't afford to think of James Thayer as a man, attractive or otherwise. She had to remember that he was her adversary. That he was the main stumbling block to her playing a pivotal role in her children's lives.

Vicky nervously nibbled on her bottom lip. Her original hope that exposure would dilute her intense sexual reaction to him wasn't working. At least, not so far. But then, she'd only been here two days. Maybe being overly aware of a man was like having a cold. Maybe it took a week or so to work its way through your system. Maybe all she had to do was hold on and by this time next week she'd be able to look at James Thayer and see nothing more than a handsome, wealthy, well-educated, superbly mannered man.

She stole a quick glance at James, her eyes lingering on his gentle smile as he listened to his aunt.

Vicky felt her stomach twist. And then again, maybe she wouldn't.

"Did you have a nice morning, Vicky?" Sophie asked. "I looked for you earlier, but I couldn't find you."

"I was in the library for most of the morning," Vicky said, "and then..."

Her voice trailed as the sun appeared, pouring through the window behind Sophie. The brilliant sunlight engulfed the elderly woman and fractured into hundreds of individual rainbows by the collection of jewelry she was wearing.

It was the most incredibly gaudy display of costume jewelry Vicky had ever seen, and she loved it. Not only was it colorful, but it was aggressively cheerful. Sophie's smiling face perched atop the display almost seemed anticlimactic.

How nice it must be to be elderly and not to worry about fashion or what other people thought about one's sartorial excesses, Vicky thought wistfully. Although, from what she'd seen of Sophie so far, Vicky doubted that she had ever cared what society thought of her.

Noticing Vicky's interest, Sophie complacently patted a large oval broach studded with oversize zircons surrounding a dull piece of red glass. Attached to the bottom of the broach were five tiny golden chains from which dangled chunks of green glass. It was almost barbaric in its excess.

"Do you like my broach?" Sophie said happily. "It was considered very avant-guarde in its time."

"The only thing that bauble was ever in avant of was bad taste," James muttered in an audible aside to Vicky.

At his unexpected comment, Vicky choked on the water she had been sipping.

"Allow me." James got to his feet and began to pound her on the back with what Vicky felt was more enthusiasm than the situation called for.

Vicky felt the warmth of his hand burning through the thin linen of her blouse. It left its imprint on the skin of her back, making it hard to think straight.

"What's wrong with the gel, James?"

A good question, Vicky thought morosely. What *was* wrong with her that just the touch of the man should send her into a state of confusion? She just wished she had an equally good answer.

"She swallowed wrong." James sat back down, deliberately picking up his own glass of water and taking a drink as if to show Vicky how it should be done.

Vicky glared at him, and the wicked gleam in his eyes deepened. Was he was making fun of her? Or was he teasing her? The possibility gave her pause. Whether he was laughing at her or with her made a big difference and, like so much else connected with this man, she didn't know.

"Modern women have no fortitude," Sophie said.

"Not that it's poor Vicky's fault, it's the way they're raised. Spare the rod and spoil the child."

"This from a woman who was never hit in her life," James said dryly.

"Certainly not," Sophie agreed complacently. "Gentleman never hit girls, and no one could ever accuse my father of not being a gentleman. Could have accused him of lots of other things, though," she added. "And a few foolhardy souls actually did."

"Her father was a robber baron who ruthlessly destroyed anyone who got in his way," James translated in an aside to Vicky.

Vicky felt an unnerving sense of companionship with James. As if the two of them were communicating on some level not apparent to anyone else.

"We had a lot of robber barons in America, too." Vicky used her words to force some distance between them. "Usually when they got old they gave away vast sums of money to charity to try to make amends."

"More likely to try to buy their way into heaven," Sophie said dryly. "At least Papa had enough sense to know that was a hopeless cause."

Vicky looked at James and almost giggled at the laughter she could see lighting his eyes. There was no doubt about it. James Thayer had a sense of humor. A sense of humor big enough to laugh at his own family. He wasn't nearly as stiff as she'd originally thought.

But just because he had a sense of humor didn't mean that he was any less determined to exclude her from her children's lives, she reminded herself. The fact that James Thayer was turning out to be a very complex man didn't change the most important thing about him. He wanted her gone. Out of her children's lives.

In a way, fighting him would be easier if he were a physically repulsive, nasty man, she thought uneasily. Then it would be easy to keep her mind on the fact that he was the enemy.

"Do you belong to the WI, dear?" Sophie asked.

Vicky glanced at James, not sure to whom the question had been directed.

"Oh, not him." Sophie caught her confused glance. "He's not eligible."

"She means I'm a man," James said.

He sure was, Vicky thought as her eyes instinctively measured the width of his shoulders. In fact, simply calling him a man didn't begin to do justice to his sex.

"WI is the Woman's Institute," Sophie explained.

"We don't have the organization where I live," Vicky said, mentally scrambling to remember exactly where the real Ms. Lascoe lived. A suburb of Philadelphia called Bala something or other, but definitely not the city proper. To her relief, Sophie didn't ask where she lived.

"I'm sure you colonials do your best," Sophie said. "You may come along with me this afternoon and see how it should be done. We are discussing plans to raise money to replace the vestry roof."

"No, thank you," Vicky hurriedly declined. She hated committee meetings. And now that James had told Nanny that Vicky was allowed to see the twins, she intended to spend as much of her time with them as she could.

"Remember to take off all those…things before you go." James gestured toward the array of costume jewelry that covered virtually every square inch of Sophie's flat chest and decorated all of her fingers.

"But I like to wear them, dear," Sophie said. "They

make me feel fancy, and at my age there isn't much left that does, you know.''

''No,'' James flatly refused.

Vicky stared down at her plate. His arbitrary order jarred loose fragments of similar edicts from her late husband. Zane had also been addicted to issuing orders about what she should or should not wear. For her entire married life she'd suffered Zane's strictures in silence and hated herself for being so spineless.

But now she was a bona fide graduate of an assertiveness training class, she reminded herself. Now she knew how to stand up for herself. She glanced down the table at Sophie's unhappy face. And for others, if need be.

She knew the technique worked. She'd used it on James just this morning when she'd forced him to let her see the twins. And every time she practiced asserting herself she would get better at it, her instructor had said.

James might be the local lord of the manor and very conscious of his position in the community, but surely it didn't matter if his great-aunt liked to deck herself out like a Christmas tree. Everyone would surely understand that it was simply an elderly woman's harmless fancy that in no way reflected on James. And even if they didn't, so what? Vicky thought militantly. They could just look the other way if their fashion sense was so outraged.

Vicky took a deep breath and jumped into the fray. ''I think she looks great. Cheerful,'' she added in the face of James's dumbfounded expression.

''Do you mean to tell me you approve of her going out in public wearing all that...''

Vicky tried to ignore the caustic edge to his voice.

She couldn't back down at the first sign of opposition or she'd wind up like before, agreeing to things she didn't want to do simply to preserve the peace. She was done with conciliation. With peace at any price. The cost was far too high.

"Jewelry." Vicky supplied the word he couldn't seem to get out. "And of course I approve. Why not?"

"Why not!" James repeated.

"I asked first," Vicky shot back, feeling her nervousness begin to fade as other, more elusive, emotions began to surface. An emotion that was almost a sense of anticipation.

"You are a guest in this house—" James began.

"No, she ain't." Sophie cackled in delight. "She's a connection. You said so yourself. Connections got rights."

"Yah." Vicky grinned happily at James as a feeling of exhilaration swept through her. They both knew what her connection to the Thayers was, and he was the one determined to keep it a secret. "Connections got rights."

"Got rights to lots of things," Sophie continued. "You seen the priest's hole yet, gel?"

"What?" Vicky blinked, completely lost at this unexpected conversational turn,

"James, never tell me you didn't show the gel our priest's hole. Why, one of his very own ancestors haunts it."

"Aunt Sophie, it does not have a ghost. The only thing that was ever spilled in there was a little communion wine, certainly not blood."

"In where?" Intrigued, Vicky looked from Sophie's belligerent face to James's exasperated one. One thing you could say about Sophie, she sure kept the conversation moving.

"In our priest's hole," Sophie explained. "Really, James, you modern youth have no imagination."

"That's quite all right, you have enough for both of us," James said.

"What is a priest's hole?" Vicky tried to redirect the conversation onto a path where she could follow it.

"After Henry the VIII outlawed Catholicism, some families built hidden rooms to hide the priests when they came to say mass," James explained. "This house has one."

"James will show it to you after lunch," Sophie decreed.

"Oh, but—" Vicky began, not wanting James to think that she was angling to spend time alone with him. It would be too humiliating.

"Save your protests," James told her. "Once Aunt Sophie decides you should do something, it's easier to just go along with it."

"I see," Vicky muttered, not seeing at all. If that were true, then why didn't he simply go along with Sophie's barbaric taste in adornment? Why try to stop her from wearing it? Unless the problem was that she wanted to wear it in public where everyone could see her. Did he care more about what other people thought than he cared about his aunt's feelings?

Vicky glanced at James, studying him beneath her lashes. Her eyes traced over his firm chin. His very firm chin. It didn't look like the chin of a man who would be swayed by public opinion.

But then, looks could be deceptive. A chill feathered through her as she remembered Zane. He'd seemed like such a nice man when she'd first met him. Such a thoughtful man. She'd seen him as the answer to all her problems, only to find that he was simply one more problem to deal with. One that had consumed virtually all her time and patience and, in the end, had threatened to consume her very identity.

"Don't look so sad, gel." Sophie's voice recalled Vicky from her memories. "James'll show you the priest's hole."

The priest's hole was the least of the things he'd like to explore with her, James thought as he studied her downbent head. It gleamed golden. His fingers tingled with the compulsion to touch it. To see if her hair was as soft as it looked. He wanted to bury his face in the silken length of it and breathe in the very faint floral scent that clung to her. He wanted to imprint her exact scent on his mind past all forgetting. He wanted…

"You will show Vicky, won't you?" His aunt's question broke into his thoughts, and he allowed his desire to drift away like the impossible dream it was.

"Yes, Aunt Sophie, I will show Vicky the priest's hole."

"Good." Sophie got to her feet. "You do that while I go take a nap before my meeting. Got to be in form, you know."

"Oh, I know." James chuckled, and the loving indulgence in his voice sent a wave of emotion through Vicky. It shouldn't have. James's relationship with his great-aunt was none of her business. All that should concern her was his relationship with her children.

"Then get to it, boy," Aunt Sophie ordered.

James obediently put down his napkin and got to his feet, hoping he didn't look as eager to get Vicky alone as he felt. He didn't have the slightest doubt that she would exploit any weakness to her client's advantage. And his children's disadvantage.

Vicky watched his face harden and wondered what was going on. One minute the indulgence he normally showed his aunt was about to lap over onto her, and then, suddenly, he'd gone all remote on her. As if he'd just discovered she was lying about her identity.

No, Vicky assured herself. There was no way he could have figured out who she was between one breath and the next. And he didn't need to figure it out. She was going to tell him. Just as soon as she'd had a chance to spend some time with her children. That way, even if he kicked her out, she would have made a start on becoming a mother in fact as well as in name.

Maybe his sudden withdrawal was nothing more than that he didn't want to waste his time showing her around his house, she thought as she followed the now-silent James out of the dining room.

The possibility didn't make her feel any better. She didn't want him to do things with her on sufferance. She wanted him to show her around because he wanted to. Although, actually, if he were going to show her anything, she'd like to see more of his art collection.

A warm flush heated the soft skin of her cheeks. If ever that old line about a man inviting a girl up to see his etchings fit a situation, this was it. And after she'd shown a perfunctory interest in his artwork, she could explore what really interested her. Him. She could wrap her arms around his lean waist and snuggle against him. She could bury her face in his broad chest and breath in the clean masculine scent of his hard body.

''It's in here.'' James's voice echoed oddly in her ears, and she blinked, struggling to reconcile the smiling, sensual James of her imagination with the impassive man staring at her.

"Are you all right?" He frowned at her.

"Yes, I was just thinking." Vicky mumbled the first excuse that came to mind.

"They must have been fascinating thoughts," James snapped. His voice had a decided edge to it that made him wince when he heard it. Vicky was his adversary and, somehow, he had to keep that thought in the forefront of his mind. He just didn't know how. Where Vicky was concerned, his emotions seemed to have an agenda that operated independently of his mind.

"I was thinking about etchings." Vicky blurted out the truth and then cringed at the thought of what he might make of it.

"Etchings?" he repeated in confusion. "If you like etchings, I have several you might find interesting. One of my ancestors was a devotee of Michelangelo, and he brought home quite a few etchings from his grand tour of Europe. I'm told they are particularly fine examples of the type."

Vicky listened to the disinterest in his voice in disbelief. The man owned Michelangelos in the plural, and his only comment was that he had been told they were fine examples of the type?

"You don't like Michelangelo's stuff?" she asked curiously.

"He's all right. I simply find his etchings rather bleak. Personally, I prefer something with a little more life to it. Like that." James gestured toward an oversize portrait hanging on the wall beside them. It depicted a gorgeous young woman from the Regency period whose lush bosom was falling out of the bodice of her ball gown.

Vicky felt a flash of irritation. Did every man think that femininity was measured by a woman's bust size? Wasn't there a man anywhere who had the sense to know that small could be just as feminine as big?

"It's too bad she used so much material for that full skirt or she might have had enough left over to make a top for that dress," Vicky snapped.

James blinked. "Does nudity offend you?" he asked.

His sure wouldn't, Vicky thought. His nudity would excite her and intrigue her and captivate her, but never offend her. Not that she was likely to ever see him without the civilizing effects of clothes. The thought depressed her and the depression scared her. What on earth was the matter with her? Her emotions had been seesawing all over the place since she'd met James.

It wasn't James himself, she assured herself. It was just that her meeting him coincided with meeting her children. It was the uncertainty surrounding what role she was to be allowed to play in their lives that was making her feel so unsettled.

"No, nudity per se doesn't bother me," she muttered. "It's just—" She ground to a halt. There was no way she could explain to him her own dissatisfaction with being a AAA bust size in a society that worshipped DDD. It would sound pathetic. Even worse, he might think she was coming on to him. That she was asking him to notice her breasts. The thought appalled her.

"Just what?" James asked.

"Just, just," she repeated dampeningly. "Where is this thing you are going to show me?" Vicky determinedly changed the subject.

To her relief he allowed her to.

"It's through there." He pointed toward a door farther down the hallway on their right.

"The doors seem smaller in this part of the house," she said as she entered the room. "Or is it my imagination?"

"No, they really are smaller. This section is the original building, and not only are the doors smaller but the floors are uneven.

"The priest's hole is over here." He headed across the room toward the large fireplace.

"I take it your family was Catholic?"

"Everyone's family was Catholic until Henry set up the Church of England. Then everyone became Anglican. Some found it easier than others."

"And then his daughter, Mary, got the throne and everybody turned back into Catholics." Vicky shook her head. "Life couldn't have been easy for anyone back then who truly believed in something."

"Life is never easy for someone who truly believes in something," James said dryly. "The only difference is that burning people at the stake is frowned upon in most of the world these days."

"There is that," she agreed.

James stopped in front of the ornately carved fireplace and studied the upper left side for a long moment.

"As I remember…" He grasped a delicately carved acorn in his lean fingers and twisted it to the left. There was a creaking noise and then a section of the paneling beside the fireplace slowly moved about eighteen inches to the left. A whiff of cold, damp air puffed into the room reminding Vicky of ghost stories and crypts. She shivered.

"What's wrong?" James caught her involuntary reaction.

"Nothing," she denied. "I was just remembering what your aunt said about the ghost of your ancestor. That hole looks like exactly the kind of place a self-respecting ghost would pick to haunt."

"Not him," James said cheerfully. "If the old boy really were a ghost, he'd have picked the wine cellar since that was his favorite place to haunt when he was alive."

Vicky giggled at James's irreverent attitude.

She ought to laugh more often, James thought as he glanced at her bright face. She looked different when she laughed. Younger, more carefree. More approachable. More trouble. The thought cooled his sudden enthusiasm.

James turned sideways, slipped between the opening and disappeared into the darkness beyond. Vicky glanced around the sunny room, took a deep breath and followed him into a tiny room no more than four feet on each side.

"Those priests must have been on the thin side," she muttered, "'cause Friar Tuck would never have fit in here."

She let out a squeak of alarm as the door closed, engulfing her in pitch-blackness. "Why'd you do that?" she demanded.

"So you can get a feel for what it would have been like to have been locked up in here. You aren't claustrophobic, are you?"

"This is a fine time to ask! And no, I'm not. At least, I don't think so. But I must say, if I had to hide out in here for any length of time I could be. You can't see anything."

"That was the whole point." James's disembodied voice came from slightly above and to her left. Instinctively she edged closer to him, seeking something alive in this strangely dead place.

"While the priest was hiding in here, the soldiers would be searching the house for him. Any betraying flicker of light or noise and he was dead. And so was the house owner who harbored him."

Vicky shuddered at the grim picture his words evoked. It was hard to think that such things had happened right here where she was standing. No wonder people believed in ghosts.

James could feel her trembling, and he wanted to take her in his arms and tell her that there was nothing to worry about. That she was safe. He took a deep breath to combat the urge, and the faintly floral fragrance of her perfume filled his lungs, valiantly fighting against the dankness of the stale air. It was as if she represented life and hope in the midst of so much old pain and death.

"Well, I can now tell your aunt I've seen the priest's hole." Vicky's voice sounded unnaturally bright to her ears, but she didn't care. She wanted out. Away from this tightly enclosed place and away from the wild torrent of emotions that being this close to James caused. She turned slightly, and a cobweb brushed across her face. A thick cobweb. A second later she felt something skitter across her cheek.

She jumped, propelled forward on a rush of terror. "There's a spider on me! I can feel it!" She hated spiders. Particularly the big hairy kind that would make such a dark, dank spot his home.

Vicky landed against James's chest, and his arms immediately closed around her. Her first reaction was relief. She felt safe in James's arms. Her breath escaped on a relieved sigh. But as she inhaled again, along with air came the purely masculine scent of his body. The spicy fragrance of his cologne, the clean smell of his white shirt and the incredibly seductive scent of his skin.

The tumultuous potpourri of smells poured through her mind, scattering her lingering terror of spiders. She was much too busy processing the essence of James to worry about insect life.

"Don't worry." James's voice sounded slightly deeper than normal in the darkness. "We don't have poisonous spiders here."

"They don't have to poison me," she muttered distractedly. "They can simply scare me to death."

James's arms tightened as he felt the tremor that shivered through her. This is a bad idea, he told himself. He should let go of her. He should open the panel and set her outside.

And he would, he promised himself. Just as soon as he comforted her. She was his guest, after all. And he had been the one to scare her. That he hadn't meant to was no excuse. The least he could do was kiss her and make it better.

Not giving himself time to consider the wisdom of what he was about to do, James lowered his head, and his lips unerringly found hers. The softness of her mouth sent a wave of reaction through him. His arms tightened instinctively, gathering her closer. When she didn't object, he increased the pressure of his mouth against hers, consumed by a burning need for more.

Stop it, his intellect screamed at him. This woman was the enemy. But his emotions made short work of his intellect. His need to taste her, to feel her body pressed against the length of his, blotted out every single rational reason why it was a bad idea.

The very faint sound Vicky made in the back of her throat was what finally broke his self-absorption. His feeling of euphoria died as suddenly as it had sprung to life, leaving him unsure of himself. Was she trying to escape him? Was she angry? She hadn't seemed to object to his kissing her, but she might have been afraid to pull away for fear of running into the spider again.

The thought mortified him, and he hastily dropped his arms and stepped back, bumping into the wall with a thump. Damn! he thought in self-disgust. She must think he was a chauvinistic jerk who had taken advantage of her momentary fright to kiss her. And the worst part of it was that it was true. He *had* taken advantage of the opportunity. Grabbed it with both hands.

Embarrassed and confused by his abnormal behavior, he reached up and turned the lever to open the door.

A feeling of loss engulfed him when she hurriedly slipped through it.

James stepped out after her and made a production of reclosing the panel while he frantically tried to think. Should he pretend that the kiss hadn't happened? Or should he apologize for it? If so, how profuse should his apology be?

He finally got the panel closed and shot a quick assessing glance at Vicky, trying to read her mood. Other than the fact that she was paler than usual, she looked normal. Was she pale because of the spider or pale with anger because he'd kissed her?

"I'm sorry," he blurted out. "I didn't mean to do that."

If that's the way he kissed when he didn't mean to do it, then God help her if he ever kissed her and meant it, Vicky thought. The experience would probably blow her mind. But since the kiss that she had found so emotionally shattering had been nothing more than an impulse to him, an impulse that he now regretted, pride demanded that she didn't let him know how shattering she had found it.

"Think nothing of it." She forced an airy note into her voice. "It was just a kiss, after all."

It wasn't just a kiss, James thought. That had been a kiss with a capital *K*. A foretaste of the sheer voluptuous indulgence that making love to her would be. To him at least. But obviously not to her. The thought made him want to throw something. How could he have been so moved, while she sounded as if nothing had happened.

Because…from her perspective nothing had happened. The truth disheartened him.

Chapter Six

Vicky felt suffocated by the thick silence that had enveloped them since they'd left the priest's hole. The kiss they'd shared seemed to have completely dried up her stock of polite small talk.

She stole a quick glance at James. He looked exactly the same as always. Clearly, kissing her hadn't been all that big a deal to him. And with good reason. A man with as much going for him as James Thayer could have his pick of gorgeous, sophisticated women. He certainly wouldn't find a thirty-year-old widow from a very ordinary background of any lasting interest. What was surprising was that he had kissed her in the first place.

But then, she had practically flung herself into his arms when she'd brushed up against that ghastly spider web. Could he have thought her fear had been an act? Could he have thought that she'd done it so he would kiss her?

Chagrin twisted through her. Surely he didn't think

she would do that, did he? It made her seem so…so pathetic. Like a woman desperate for physical contact with a man. And she wasn't. It was her choice not to have a man in her life. The only emotional ties she wanted to foster were those between herself and her children. Children she could cope with. Children she could reasonably hope to understand. Men were a whole other ball game, and she wasn't willing to pay the price of admission again.

Vicky took a deep breath, determined to do something to relieve the oppressive silence. Something that would return their relationship to what it had been before that devastating kiss. She searched her mind for a clever, witty comment about something, anything.

By the time they reached the top of the grand staircase on the second floor, she had given up on witty or clever and was willing to settle for anything that was even vaguely coherent.

"I think I'll go see the twins," she finally blurted out.

"They take a nap in the afternoon."

"If they're asleep, I won't stay, but you did say that I could have access to them whenever I wanted," she reminded him, worried that he'd changed his mind.

"And I meant it, but…"

"I'd feel a lot better about your assurance if you hadn't ended it with *but,*" Vicky said.

"It isn't that I don't want you to see the twins," he began.

"I promise I won't harm them."

"I know you wouldn't, at least not intentionally."

"It isn't easy to accidentally hurt a child, provided you use common sense." Vicky quoted the baby book she'd been studying ever since she'd found out she was a mother. "Babies are a lot sturdier than they look."

"You should have seen them right after they were born." His voice hardened. "They were three weeks premature and had a great deal of trouble breathing on their own."

"That was then. This is now. Now they look very healthy."

"They are," James agreed. "And one of the reasons they are so healthy is because of Nanny. She has done a remarkable job."

"I can see that." Vicky gave credit where it was due.

"Then why can't you see that I don't want to upset her by pushing too hard too fast? What will I do if she leaves?"

"I'll…" Vicky hurriedly corrected herself. "Their mother will take care of them."

"Mrs. Sutton?" he repeated incredulously.

"It's not that revolutionary a concept," Vicky said dryly. "Women all over the world take care of their own children. And most of them do it because they want to."

The women he'd known certainly hadn't wanted to, James thought. His own mother had turned him over to a nanny the minute he'd been born and had only seen him a couple times a year after that. And Romayne hadn't even waited for the twins to get out of intensive care before she'd signed away all her rights to them in her eagerness to rush their divorce. Maybe the women in Vicky's world cared for their own children, but the women in his sure didn't.

"Does Mrs. Sutton have any experience with children?'' James asked, wondering what it was about the woman that inspired such loyalty in Vicky.

"No.'' Vicky opted for the truth. She'd already told James so many lies she was having trouble remembering them all.

"Then how can you even suggest her taking over from Nanny?''

"It's easy. She's their mother. She loves them. Love makes up for a lot of deficiencies. Besides, parenting is a hands-on learning experience.'' Vicky quoted the baby book again.

"So are lots of other activities such as bank robbery and murder,'' he said dryly.

"I refuse to be drawn into a fallacious argument. You said I could have access to the twins, and I intend to hold you to it.''

"I have no intention of going back on my word. I simply want you to…'' He gestured impotently.

"Say yes and amen to everything Attila the Nanny says?'' Vicky filled in the blank.

"Don't call her that!''

"Why not? It seems pretty appropriate to me.''

"Because you might accidentally say it to her face.''

"I'm far more likely to say it to her face *on purpose* if she doesn't back off a little,'' Vicky snapped.

James pressed his lips together in frustration. In his heart he agreed with Vicky. Nanny was a martinet. But she was a martinet who was doing a great job. If she got mad and quit— What would he do? What would the twins do?

Now, if Vicky were the one offering to stay and take care of them, he might be tempted. She was a calm, sensible woman who clearly cared about the twins' well-being. But Vicky was a highly trained lawyer with a demanding career. She didn't have the time to care for two babies. The wonder of it was that she had managed to free up enough time to come to England in the first place.

"I'll come with you," he finally said with the vague idea of somehow keeping the peace between Nanny and Vicky. And he could see the twins again, he thought on a burst of anticipation. Even if they were asleep. He hadn't watched them sleep since those horrible first weeks in the hospital when he'd hung over them all hours of the day and night willing them to live.

"Sure," Vicky agreed. "You're their father."

Yes, he was their father. And a singularly stupid one he'd turned out to be. If he'd had any sense when he'd picked out a wife, their mother would have been someone like…like Vicky Lascoe. Someone who was prepared to love the twins for themselves. Someone who didn't banish her children to the nursery so she wouldn't have to be bothered with them.

Hindsight is always twenty-twenty, he told himself. And he could honestly say he'd learned from his first marriage. He would never again be trapped by a rush of hormones. Now he had more sense.

He looked down at Vicky, his eyes lingering on the delicate line of her cheekbone. At least, he hoped he did.

When they reached the nursery, James lifted his hand to knock on the closed door.

"You don't have to knock," Vicky said. "This is your house and those are your kids."

Reaching around him, she turned the knob, pushed the door open and walked inside.

James followed her a little more cautiously. He

didn't want to wake the children if they were already asleep.

They weren't, he realized, as he took in the open-mouthed stare of the nursery maid who was holding a thick, fluffy towel in her hand.

"Yes?" Nanny spoke from behind them. "I am bathing the twins before their nap instead of after since you allowed Edmond to get as much cereal on him as in him."

"We'll help." Vicky ignored the criticism.

"Help!" Nanny squawked.

"That's what I said." Vicky took the towel out of the maid's limp fingers, plucked Edmond out of his bath and wrapped the towel around his chubby little body.

"You dry him while I wash Mary Rose," Vicky told James.

James took an eager step toward his son only to stop when Nanny said, "You might drop him, sir. Wet babies are very slippery."

"So sit on the floor and dry him, James." Vicky handed Edmond to him.

James took his son, holding him with the same exaggerated care one might hold a live grenade.

"But—" Nanny sputtered.

"That way Edmond won't have far to fall if James does drop him," Vicky told Nanny with determined cheerfulness.

Taking Vicky's directive literally, James sat down on the thick green carpet and began to carefully dry Edmond's small body.

Vicky felt something twist in her chest at James's expression. He looked so endearingly earnest. And so worried about making a mistake.

Her eyes narrowed as a sudden gust of anger shook her. That blasted nanny had a lot to answer for. The woman had made James afraid to touch his own children. But Nanny wasn't going to get away with it anymore, Vicky vowed. She wouldn't let her. And if Nanny couldn't adjust to the new order, Nanny could take a hike. The sooner, the better.

Determinedly Vicky turned to Mary Rose who was sitting in a playpen wearing a diaper and a thoughtful expression.

"Hello, angel." Vicky smiled at her daughter and felt like bursting with pride when Mary Rose smiled back. Mary Rose knew who loved her.

"Have you ever bathed a baby, madame?" Nanny demanded.

"Nope, this will be my first time. Just like you had a first time."

Vicky ignored the strangled sound from the maid.

"I was trained," Nanny insisted.

"I think the point Ms. Lascoe is making," James said unexpectedly from his spot on the floor, "is that baby care is learned."

Vicky gave him an encouraging smile. That sounded far more like the James she had first encountered than the nervous father Nanny had so carefully kept under her thumb.

Nanny subsided like a pricked balloon at James's words and simply stood there with her arms crossed watching intently while Vicky carefully bathed her daughter.

Vicky never even noticed. Nothing mattered to her at the moment but the chance to be a real mother to her daughter. To do one of the simple, everyday things that she should have been doing since Mary Rose's

birth. Things that she hoped to be doing for a long time
to come.

Once Vicky had Mary Rose dressed in the soft, knit
nighty that Nanny shoved at her, she spent a precious
few seconds cuddling the little girl. She wanted to trade
twins with James for a moment so she could also hug
Edmond, but she was afraid James might wonder why,
and she could hardly tell him the truth in front of
Nanny. She needed privacy to confess her real identity.
And privacy for his response. He wasn't going to like
having been fooled. But then she hadn't liked the ne-
cessity of having to do it. And, if he had been the least
bit reasonable about allowing her to visit in the first
place, she wouldn't have had to resort to impersonation.

But why she had done it didn't matter anymore. It
was time to tell him and clear the air. She just hoped
that it *would* clear the air and not get her kicked out.

"It is time for the twins to nap," Nanny's firm voice
interrupted her thoughts.

Vicky handed Mary Rose to Nanny, watching hun-
grily as Nanny carefully placed the sleepy baby in her
white crib and covered her with a pale pink blanket.
Nanny then retrieved Edmond from his father, who
handed him over with an obvious reluctance that elicited a chord of sympathy from Vicky.

How nice it would be if there were no nanny, Vicky
thought. If there were just the twins and her and James.
If they were just a normal family… But they weren't.
She hastily stifled the errant thought. She might make
a pretty normal, run-of-the-mill mother, but there was
nothing normal about James. Not his aristocratic background, not his wealth, not his looks and certainly not

his personality. About the only thing James had in common with the men she'd known was his sex.

"If you would leave, the twins can take their nap, otherwise we will be cranky tonight," Nanny said.

She had a news flash for Nanny, Vicky thought, annoyed at the woman's use of the royal *we*. She didn't know about the twins, but Nanny had been nothing but cranky since Vicky had arrived. In fact, it was a wonder that the twins were so even-tempered with a primary caregiver who seemed to be in a perpetual snit.

Although, maybe it was simply that she had disrupted the woman's normal routine. Vicky tried to be fair. Maybe Nanny was not a person who dealt with change very well. If so, she was in for a decided shock when Vicky finally wrested partial custody of the babies from James. Vicky had no intention of allowing the woman to dictate to her.

"That went very well," James said once Nanny had managed to maneuver them out into the hallway and close the nursery door behind them. "Much better than I thought it would."

"You're an intelligent, competent man, James. Why shouldn't you transfer that competence to your children?"

James felt a surge of confidence at Vicky's matter-of-fact words. What was there about this woman that made him feel he really could deal with the twins? Maybe it was her profession? Maybe lawyers learned in school how to inspire confidence?

He frowned slightly. Maybe, but when he thought about it, she was the oddest lawyer he'd ever met. She never talked about the law in general or the cases she'd handled in particular. Was it discretion on her part or disinterest?

She'd certainly been enthusiastic about her hobby. She'd been more than willing to talk about it. He remembered her very real outrage over the corruption of the Latin language during the Middle Ages.

It didn't make any sense. Why would she invest so much time and energy into becoming a lawyer if she didn't like it? He didn't know, and he wanted to. He wanted to know all about her.

"I've noticed you don't talk much about being a lawyer," he probed.

Vicky took a deep breath. He'd just given her the perfect opening for her to confess who she was. She could tell him right now and get it over with. Or, better still, tell him and then run like the devil to hide out somewhere until he had a chance to calm down.

"No, I don't," she mumbled as she tried to think of the best way to word her confession. Should she just blurt out the truth or lead up to it gracefully? But what was the graceful way to tell someone you'd been lying to them?

"I find it hard to think of you as a lawyer," James continued. "You don't seem like the type to corner someone and wring a confession out of him."

"I'm not," she muttered. "I find the law confusing and disheartening. And damned unfair." Her voice hardened slightly as she remembered the law's ambiguous response to her perfectly reasonable request to see her own children.

"Then why do you stay in it?" James asked.

"Well, I don't... I mean... The law..." Vicky scrambled to find the words to make him understand why she'd lied. "I'm not...I'm connected to the twins," she finally got out a complete sentence.

"Connected?" James's voice hardened further, rattling her composure.

"As in related," Vicky offered, watching him nervously to see how he took her confession.

Related? So that explained his sense of having seen her before, James realized. His subconscious mind had noticed her resemblance to his children even if his conscious mind hadn't. But if she was related to the twins, then she was also related to Mrs. Sutton. Which explained why a busy lawyer would take the time to come to England and assess the emotional and physical development of her client's children. But just how close a relation to Mrs. Sutton was Vicky?

"Are you a cousin of Mrs. Sutton's?" James asked, trying to decide if Vicky's being related to the woman was good news or bad. Would her family loyalty blind her to the fact that it was best for the twins to remain with him where they were thriving? He didn't know. Nor did he have enough personal experience with families to even hazard a guess.

"No." Vicky got out part of the truth.

"Then you must be what Aunt Sophie calls a connection." James drew his own conclusions. "As near as I can tell, the way she uses the word, it encompasses everyone from godparents to cousins sixteen times removed."

"Well, I'm not sixteen times removed from the twins' mother," Vicky began.

"Who is an American," James threw in.

"What?" Vicky blinked, confused by the nonsequitur.

"Mrs. Sutton is an American."

"Yes, but she and I are…are…" Vicky choked on the words *the same person*.

"Americans." James followed his own line of thought. "And while there's nothing wrong with Americans…"

"Let me guess, some of your best friends are Americans?" she said acidly.

"Actually, no." James totally missed her sarcasm. "Although I do admire Americans' inventiveness as well as their willingness to pitch in and help when it's needed.

"But the point I am making is that the twins are English, not Americans."

"How did you reach that conclusion?" Vicky demanded. "They have as much English blood in them as they do American."

"They were born in England."

"They were conceived in America, but why were they?" Vicky asked the question she'd wanted to ask ever since she'd found out the doctor had forged her name on the release form and sold her eggs to James and his wife. "England has good clinics. Why go all the way to New York to have the procedure done?"

"Anonymity," James said succinctly. "I didn't want to risk some reporter from the gutter press stumbling across the facts and embarrassing the twins later on. But no matter where they were conceived, the twins were born in England and that makes them English. They should be raised in England."

Away from their American mother. Vicky mentally finished the sentence for him. Which, thanks to her dithering, he still thought was the unknown Mrs. Sutton.

But she'd tried, Vicky told herself. If he hadn't sidetracked her with his comment about nationality…

She'd probably still be trying to figure out how to

word her confession, she admitted truthfully. The plain fact was that she was afraid to do anything that would upset her tentative position in his household.

And it wasn't even a question of utilizing her assertiveness training skills, she realized. It wasn't exactly that she was afraid to tell him. It was that she was afraid to deal with the results of telling him.

"The twins' mother has every right to know her children. And, conversely, the twins have a right to a mother's love," Vicky finally said.

James was caught off balance by her assertion. Could Vicky be right? Would there come a day when the twins would regret not having a mother? Would they blame him for that lack?

But even if Vicky were right about them needing a mother's love, it didn't mean that Mrs. Sutton was the only woman who could adequately mother them. He remembered how lovingly Vicky had held Mary Rose. Vicky would make a great mother.

"You might not like it, James, but Mrs. Sutton is the twins' mother. She has as much right to raise them as you do."

"They are English," he insisted.

"All right, so they're English," she said impatiently. "I'll concede their nationality because it doesn't much matter what national label someone sticks on them. What matters is what kind of people they grow up to be."

"You've already told me Mrs. Sutton doesn't have any experience at raising children," James snapped, irrationally annoyed at the way she kept pushing Mrs. Sutton's claim to the twins.

"How much have you had?"

"Nanny—"

"So you admit that it's Nanny who is raising them?" Vicky demanded.

"The twins are babies. They need specialized care."

"The twins are babies who need to be loved by their parents. Nanny is not a parent."

"I love them!"

"I'll concede that, if you'll tell me why you think their mother doesn't."

"She's never even met them."

"Not for lack of trying! You're the one who's stymied her attempts to play any part in their lives so far."

James studied Vicky's tight features with a feeling of intense frustration. Why couldn't he make her understand? Make her give up her misplaced loyalty to Mrs. Sutton in favor of doing the best thing for Edmond and Mary Rose.

"I refuse to even discuss them leaving my house!" he said.

"What you want will not be the final word in this. Their mother—"

"I beg your pardon, sir, but you have a phone call from Singapore. They said it was important."

Both James and Vicky jerked around in shock at the unexpected sound of Beech's impassive voice.

Damn, Vicky thought in frustration. One couldn't even have a fight in this house without someone overhearing. It was like living in a fishbowl.

"I'll be right there," James snapped, and Beech hastily left, looking glad to escape the line of fire.

"We have not finished this discussion," James said over his shoulder as he followed Beech's retreating figure.

"You'd better believe it," Vicky muttered.

Slowly she turned and headed toward the back of

the house, intending on escaping into the gardens for a while. She needed time to think and plan her next move. So far she wasn't doing too well at improvising.

To her relief Vicky made it into the gardens without meeting a soul. She didn't want to talk to anyone at the moment. She wanted to think about James's insistence on the twins being English. Think about whether her giving in on that point might encourage him to think she would give in on other points. Such as, her right to see them on a regular basis.

She collapsed into a white lounger behind a huge copper beech tree and closed her eyes in order to think more clearly. She promptly fell asleep.

It was the sound of Nanny's voice that finally woke her.

Vicky opened her eyes and peered blearily around. The sound was coming from the other side of the privet hedge to her left.

Vicky frowned slightly, trying to make out the words. She couldn't. They sounded like nonsense syllables.

She glanced down at her watch, shocked to realize that three hours had passed since she'd left James. She must have been more tired than she'd thought to have slept like that.

Curious, she got to her feet and followed the sound of Nanny's voice around the hedge to find the woman herself. She was sitting on a red plaid blanket. In front of her were the twins. Edmond was on his stomach trying to figure out how to crawl while Mary Rose was lying on her back studiously investigating her toes.

A smile curved Vicky's lips at the sight. A smile that turned thoughtful as she listened to Nanny break off the nursery rhyme she was singing to encourage

Edmond in his efforts to move himself. The voice Nanny was using with the twins was not the same sharp, impatient one the woman used with her. Maybe…

Vicky's thoughts were suspended as Nanny turned. Her expression soured when she saw Vicky.

"Good afternoon," Vicky said, trying to be civil.

"Madame." Nanny nodded condescendingly. "I am airing the twins."

"So I see." Without waiting for an invitation, which Vicky was certain would never be forthcoming, she sank down on the edge of the blanket.

"Edmond seems to be learning to crawl," Vicky observed.

"They aren't born knowing how to do it," Nanny said. "They must develop the proper muscle coordination first. It takes practice."

"Has Mary Rose started to crawl yet?" Vicky risked a question.

"Not yet, but she will in her own time," Nanny added as if she were afraid the question was a criticism of Mary Rose.

"The important thing is to allow them the opportunity to move freely," Nanny continued.

So keep your hands off them. Vicky had no trouble translating the sentence.

But she didn't really mind. For the moment it was enough to be this close to her children. It was so peaceful there.

Vicky looked around the velvety carpet of grass, her eyes narrowing slightly as she saw a woman emerge from behind the greenhouse and start toward the house. A path that would bring her directly by them.

Curious, Vicky studied the woman. She looked to be

somewhere in her mid-thirties, and she was wearing what Vicky immediately recognized as a designer suit. A very expensive designer suit. It was not the kind of outfit someone working for a living could afford. Which ruled out her being on the staff here. So who was she?

Vicky shot a furtive look at Nanny to find her also watching the woman approach. It was impossible to tell anything from the blankness of Nanny's expression.

"Who are you and what are you doing with Mr. Thayer's children?" the woman demanded the second she was within shouting distance.

Vicky suppressed the childish impulse to ask what business it was of hers, and replied politely, "I'm Vicky Lascoe, and I'm enjoying the air with the twins."

"Does Mr. Thayer know you are here?"

"Why don't you go ask him?" Vicky's politeness was beginning to fray.

"Don't you think I won't!" the woman snapped. "Nanny, don't you think it's time to take the twins inside?"

"No," Nanny said flatly, even though it was clear to Vicky, at least, that the woman's question had really been an order. "They haven't had their proper airing yet."

Vicky looked from the woman's furious expression to Nanny's closed one and wondered if Nanny had refused on general principles or if she'd refused because she didn't like the woman. A feeling that would have certainly been understandable. Vicky had only laid eyes on her a few minutes ago, and she already couldn't stand her.

"Mr. Thayer—" the woman began.

"If you are looking for James, I suggest you try the house," Vicky cut off the woman's harsh tone as Mary Rose's little face took on a worried look. Instinctively Vicky picked up her daughter and held her comfortingly close. To Vicky's delight, Mary Rose's expression lightened.

"James!" the woman repeated in outrage. "His name is Mr. Thayer."

"A rose by any other name," Vicky muttered. "You are upsetting his children. Please take your carping elsewhere."

The woman was so angry she sputtered. With a furious glare at Vicky's unrepentant features, she ground out, "Do you have any idea who I am?"

"Yes, you are the woman who is upsetting the children. Other than that, I don't give a damn."

"We'll see about that!" The woman turned on the heel of one of her handmade Italian leather shoes and stalked off toward the house with Vicky still not knowing who she was.

A girlfriend of James? Vicky felt a chill feather through her. But only because the woman would make James a frightful wife. And, even worse, she'd make the twins a ghastly stepmother.

Vicky watched as the woman disappeared into the house. That woman was plain bad news. But bad news on what level? The sooner she found out, the better.

Chapter Seven

"James, there you are."

James looked up at the sound of Esmee's voice, hoping the annoyance he felt at the interruption wasn't apparent in his expression.

"I'm sorry, sir." Beech followed Esmee into James's study.

"I tried to tell Miss Defoe that you left orders not to be disturbed, but—"

"And I told him that those orders hardly applied to me," Esmee said archly.

"It's all right, Beech." He dismissed the butler, knowing full well that the only way Beech could have stopped Esmee would have been by brute strength. James had known Esmee his entire life and never once had she deviated from her firm conviction that the rules applied to other people, not to her.

"I told the stupid old man it was fine." Esmee perched on the edge of James's mahogany desk.

"Beech is neither old nor stupid," James said, hoping that the door had muffled the penetrating sound of Esmee's voice.

"Really, James," she said in exasperation. "Loyalty is all well and good, but don't let it blind you to reality."

"I won't," James said dryly. "To what do I owe this..." about to say interruption, he thought better of the impulse and substituted "...visit."

"When I was in the village this morning I heard that you had some woman staying with you, and I came over to see. James, who is she? And what was she doing with the twins?"

"She's a distant relative from America who is researching her family tree. As for what she's doing with the twins, I would imagine she was playing with them. Americans are known for being fond of children."

"Notorious for it, you mean! American children are the most spoiled brats in the world. But never mind that. Whatever possessed you?"

"Esmee, if you insist on cross-examining me, at least give me a few clues as to what you're talking about."

"Cross-examine!" Esmee gave him a reproachful look. "I am trying to help you. You can't possible believe that...woman is related to you. Clearly, it is just a ruse to gain entrance to Thayer House. Why, for all you know, she could be planning to kidnap the twins."

Vicky might like to, James conceded honestly. Kidnap them and take them straight to Mrs. Sutton. But she never would. Vicky not only had too much integrity to ever do anything so underhanded, but also too much intelligence to think she could get away with it.

"I am quite certain Vicky Lascoe is exactly who she says she is."

"Well, I'm not!" Esmee said darkly.

James bit back the urge to say something very rude, reminding himself that not only was Esmee an old friend who had his best interests at heart, but also that the Thayers and the Defoes had been interconnected by friendship and marriage for over three hundred years. He just wished Esmee would find herself a husband and spend her time running *his* life.

"You'll see I'm right," Esmee predicted. "That woman has a sly look."

An image of Vicky as she had bathed Mary Rose flashed through James's mind. Her face had been tense with concentration as she'd worked so carefully. Vicky was one of the least sly people he'd ever met, but trying to convince Esmee of it would be a total waste of time. Esmee never listened to anyone else's opinion. Only to her own.

"Fortunately for you I don't have plans for this evening," Esmee announced. "I can stay for dinner and get to the bottom of this."

"That's not necessary," James began.

"I could hardly do less for a friend of such longstanding." Esmee gave him a simpering smile that set his teeth on edge. "Really, James, you are so naive where women are concerned."

"Oh, I wouldn't say that." James's voice hardened, and Esmee hastily backtracked.

"I'll just go see what Cook is planning to serve," Esmee said.

"Oh, hell!" James muttered to the back of the door as it closed behind her. The situation hardly needed Esmee Defoe playing detective. But short of ordering her off the grounds of Thayer House, there was no way to get rid of her. The woman was totally oblivious to hints. And she meant well, he told himself, trying hard to believe it.

Unsettled by the whole situation, which he seemed powerless to resolve, James got to his feet and walked over to the window. He looked outside and then leaned closer to the window when he saw Vicky walking across the lawn. She was carrying one of the twins while, beside her, Nanny pushed the pram containing the other twin.

He watched appreciatively as the late-afternoon sunlight glinted on her blond head creating a reddish aura around her. Rather like a halo, he thought fancifully, although there was nothing otherworldly about her figure. His eyes dropped down her slim length. She was most definitely a woman of this world. And the thoughts she raised in him had nothing ethereal about them. In fact, they were downright earthy, he thought wryly. He wanted to sweep her up in his arms and kiss her again. He wanted to feel the soft, yielding warmth of her mouth against his. He wanted to savor the essence of Vicky Lascoe. He shifted restlessly as his body began to react to his thoughts.

But what he wanted to do and what he could and should do were two entirely different matters. Vicky Lascoe's loyalties were given to the other side. She'd never do anything disloyal to her…whatever her exact relationship to the unknown Mrs. Sutton was. And he was pretty sure that Vicky would classify making love to him as a conflict of interest.

James sighed. He had been born in the wrong century. If he'd been one of his ancestors, say the notorious Peregrine Thayer, he could simply have kidnapped Vicky and kept her captive until she…

Until she what? he mocked. Until she fell in love with him and wanted to stay of her own accord? Not bloody likely. Women didn't fall in love with him. With his possessions, yes, but not with him. Even his own wife had ditched him the minute she'd come up with a man who could match him financially. More than likely, any woman his ancestor would have kidnapped would have stayed not because she fell in love, but because she got pregnant and had no other options, given the mores of the time. Probably they would have settled into a kind of armed neutrality where the husband got sex and she got to be mistress of a great house.

James shuddered at the bleakness of the image. As fascinating as he found Vicky, he'd rather never make love to her than have her on sufferance. He either wanted her as a willing partner to their lovemaking or he didn't want her at all.

Vicky paused outside the doors to the drawing room and surreptitiously brushed the shoulders of her green silk dress, wanting to make sure there weren't any hairs clinging to the sleek material. She wasn't trying to look good for James, she assured herself. She simply wanted to match the magnificence of her surroundings.

Walking into the drawing room, Vicky came to a halt when she saw who was sitting across from Sophie. The unpleasant woman who had taken exception to Vicky's playing with the twins.

What was she doing here? Vicky wondered. More important, who was she…besides someone who felt she had a right to vet James's houseguests? Could this

woman be the reason for James's divorce? Vicky wondered, and then dismissed the idea.

Whatever this woman's present relationship with
James, she hadn't caused his divorce. Vicky had seen
pictures of James's wife and Romayne was drop-dead
gorgeous. Any man who would trade in Romayne for
a horsy-looking, shrill-voiced nag was nuts. And whatever else James might be, he certainly wasn't stupid.

"You eat with the family?" The woman launched
an opening salvo.

"Why not, she's one of the family." Sophie spoke
up. "Not only that, but she was invited."

Vicky watched the angry flush that mottled the
woman's slightly sallow skin. Now, that was interesting, Vicky thought. Sophie clearly didn't like the
woman. Curiouser and curiouser.

"I don't believe we've been introduced." Vicky
glanced at Sophie, expecting her to do the honors.

Typically, Sophie didn't do the expected. "Let her
introduce herself," Sophie grumbled. "Just like she invited herself to dinner."

"I am James's guest!" the woman bit out. Turning
to Vicky, she said, "I am Esmee Defoe."

Vicky blinked at the woman's tone of voice, half
expecting a chorus of amens to follow the announcement. Obviously, the woman expected her to be impressed, but Vicky had no clue as to why. Could she
be romantically involved with James? Could she have
expected that James would have mentioned her? Vicky
felt her stomach lurch at the thought.

"Good evening, Miss Defoe. It is miss, isn't it?"
Vicky probed.

"For the time being." Esmee gave an annoying
smirk.

"Time being relative," Sophie muttered obscurely from her spot on the sofa.

"Are you a neighbor?" Vicky threw into the lengthening silence.

"I find it hard to believe that James hasn't mentioned me," Esmee stated.

"Your name has not come up," Vicky murmured, beginning to have a great deal of sympathy for Sophie. If she had to put up with Esmee on a regular basis, the wonder wasn't that Sophie was rude to her, the wonder was that Sophie hadn't murdered her.

"Yours has," Esmee said.

Vicky stifled a childish urge to say something rude. What was it about the woman that seemed to turn her every sentence into a challenge?

"Ah, there you are, dear boy." Sophie greeted James as he hurried into the drawing room.

"Sorry I'm late, but I was talking to a young man in Liverpool who's trying to find funding for a fascinating idea."

"Nothing fascinating has ever come out of Liverpool," Esmee decreed.

"Wasn't that where the Beatles came from?" Vicky said.

"I hardly keep up with pop groups. The classics are more to my taste. There's something so common about these pop groups. Isn't that right, James?" Esmee said.

Vicky wanted to smack the supercilious expression off Esmee's thin face, and the very violence of Vicky's reaction worried her. She'd run across overbearing, rude people before and managed to breeze through the time she'd been forced to interact with them. So why was she having this visceral reaction to Esmee Defoe? Because the woman had the potential to be an influence on her children, Vicky told herself. That was the reason she was reacting so badly. Any rational woman would cringe at the thought of her children learning social behavior from this snob.

"Whatever you think about the Beatles, Esmee, they weren't common," James said.

"Oh, well, money!" Esmee snorted in dismissal.

"Actually, I was thinking of their songs," James said mildly. "I always liked 'Eleanor Rigby' and the one about the 'Yellow Submarine.'"

"'Let It Be' was my favorite," Vicky said. "Although I'm still waiting for some of the answers."

James chuckled, and the sound slid soothingly over Vicky's prickly nerves, isolating them for a brief moment in a world of their own.

"I have all of their original releases on phonograph records," James said. "I'll play 'Let it Be' for you some evening, and you can tell me if you think it is better than the subsequent versions that were released on CD."

"Why, that sounds lovely," Esmee began brightly.

"I wouldn't dream of subjecting you to the Beatles' music when you so clearly dislike it, Esmee," James said flatly.

Vicky blinked, wondering if he really intended to play the original record for her or if he had just said it to get back at Esmee. But for what? Vicky stifled a sigh. She felt as if she'd wandered into the third act of a play without a rundown of the first two acts. She was seeing all the surface action, but the motivations were totally over her head.

"Dinner is served, sir." Beech's stentorian tones broke into her thoughts.

"Thank you, Beech."

Esmee took James's arm in a proprietary manner that infuriated Vicky. The blasted woman acted as if she owned him.

"Would you help me into the dining room, dear boy?" Sophie murmured. "I'm feeling a little frail this evening."

Vicky swallowed a grin. So she wasn't the only one annoyed at Esmee's manner. But unlike Vicky, Sophie could do something about it.

"Certainly, Aunt Sophie." James left the frustrated Esmee without a sign of regret. Carefully, taking his aunt's arm, he escorted her into the dining room, followed by the fuming, but mercifully silent, Esmee.

Vicky trailed along behind the trio, not relishing the coming meal. Esmee Defoe's presence seemed to guarantee acute indigestion.

"So, you claim to be related to the family, Miss Lascoe." Esmee launched her inquisition over the first course.

Caught unawares, Vicky choked on a vegetable in her soup.

"James, quick. This is your chance to try out the Heimlich maneuver Nanny taught us!" Sophie said.

"I hardly think we need go that far, Aunt Sophie."

James got to his feet and firmly patted Vicky on the back. She wasn't sure what he intended to accomplish, but his action certainly diverted her from the fact that she was choking. Her whole universe had inexplicably narrowed to the feel of his hard fingers burning through the thin silk of her dress, to warmth seeping into her skin and flowing along her nerve endings, thoroughly disrupting her normal common sense. She couldn't seem to form a single coherent thought that wasn't connected to the feel of him touching her.

If just his touch through her clothes was this fantastic, what would it feel like if he were to touch her bare skin?

Vicky involuntarily sucked in her breath at the tantalizing thought and swallowed the bit of veggie clogging her throat.

"Are you all right, dear?" Sophie half rose in her seat. "James, maybe you really ought to—"

"No," Vicky muttered. "I'm fine, Sophie. Really. I just swallowed wrong."

"No doubt you were listening to the conversation," James murmured from his spot behind her. "A little judicious deafness goes a long way when my aunt and Esmee meet."

Vicky gasped at the unexpectedness of his whispered words. Hastily she glanced across the large table where Esmee was glaring at her, but the woman didn't appear to have heard.

Vicky stole a quick glance at James as he returned to his seat at the head of the table.

What exactly had he meant by that? That he knew his aunt and Esmee loathed each other? But if he knew it, why had he invited Esmee to dinner? Because he wanted her here? Or because he thought an invitation was necessary because she was a neighbor? Or could he not have invited her at all as Sophie had intimated? Esmee certainly appeared to be capable of inviting herself.

But even if Esmee had invited herself, James was perfectly capable of saying no. He said it all the time to Vicky when it came to the twins. So why didn't he say no to Esmee?

Vicky felt like screaming in sheer frustration. For

every fact she turned up about James Thayer, she found herself with half a dozen more questions.

"I didn't see you at the WI meeting this afternoon, Esmee," Sophie said.

"I was busy," Esmee said.

"We decided to have a jumble sale to raise money to help the Wickhams repair their cottage," Sophie said. "What are you going to donate?"

"Nothing," Esmee sniffed. "If the Wickhams had bought fire insurance like any responsible person, they wouldn't have to go begging to their neighbors."

"They aren't begging!" Sophie said. "They don't know anything about our plans."

"They should have bought fire insurance," Esmee repeated. "You're being overly sentimental and allowing yourself to be used."

Vicky felt a flash of anger at Esmee's scathing denunciation of Sophie's desire to help the Wickhams, whoever the Wickhams were.

Quickly reviewing what her assertiveness training instructor had said about handling verbal bullies, Vicky jumped into the fray.

"Surely Sophie and her friends' desire to help a neighbor should be applauded, not condemned," Vicky said. "As for the lack of insurance, perhaps the Wickhams felt they couldn't afford the premiums."

"Helping them rewards their stupidity," Esmee announced. "Sophie is being very shortsighted."

"Sophie has seen a great deal more of both the world and human nature than either you or I have," Vicky said. "If she thinks that the Wickhams deserve help, that's good enough for me."

Vicky glanced over at James and, to her astonishment, he gave her a grin that sent all kinds of emotions rushing through her.

Mesmerized, she stared into his eyes, which were sparkling with emotion. But with what emotion? she wondered. Was James pleased with her defense of his aunt or was it something else entirely? She didn't know, but the one thing she was sure of was that Romayne was nuts to have divorced him.

The better Vicky got to know him, the more convinced she was that James Thayer had everything a woman could possibly want in a man. He was handsome, wealthy, had social position, liked children, was intelligent with a wide variety of interests, and as for sex appeal…

She glanced down at her plate as a surge of heat sent a flush over her whole body. The man positively oozed sex appeal. All he had to do was look at her, and every feminine instinct she had went on red alert. Kissing him had redefined her sense of femininity. What making love to him would be like…

It would be a very bad idea, she told herself. This wasn't about James and her. This was about the mother and father of the twins. She absolutely couldn't allow herself to be sidetracked by the man himself… Although, there was nothing wrong with finding out why his first marriage had failed, Vicky rationalized. It could be important for understanding what he might do in the future, regarding a second marriage.

Inadvertently her eyes strayed to Esmee's smugly self-satisfied features. Esmee Defoe as her children's stepmother didn't bear thinking about. But what choice did she have? The obvious truth depressed her. If James refused to listen to her complaints about Nanny, he would hardly be likely to listen to any complaints she might have about the woman he loved and wanted to marry.

Speculatively Vicky's gaze went from Esmee's petulant features to James's thoughtful expression as he listened intently to something his aunt was saying. Surely an intelligent man like James wouldn't be taken in by a nasty piece of work like Esmee Defoe? Or would he? Maybe she was different when the two of them were alone?

A scalding burst of emotion flashed through her at the very thought of Esmee alone with James.

"And what do you do for a living, Ms. Lascoe?" Esmee's voice broke into Vicky's tormented thoughts. "Or don't you want to talk about what you do?"

"Not at the dinner table," Vicky murmured.

"Quite right," Sophie spoke up. "People who prose on about their jobs are bores. And as for people who interrogate their fellow guests..." Sophie eyed Esmee over the top of her glasses.

"Sophie, you are so unworldly." Esmee dismissed the comment while Vicky wondered what it would take to puncture the blasted woman's monumental self-confidence.

"Since when have good manners been considered unworldly?" Sophie demanded.

Before Esmee could retaliate, James changed the subject.

"I had a phone call this afternoon, Esmee, from Herr Murchin," he said. "He's ready to commit to building a branch of his pharmaceutical company here in the village."

"What!" Esmee yelped.

"James said," Sophie began.

"I know what he said. I simply don't understand

why he would say it. We certainly don't want some company building a factory in our village."

"Why not?" Vicky asked curiously.

"Because it will destroy the tone of the village," Esmee retorted. "Not that I would expect an American to understand a concept like tone."

"Tone is all well and good," James said, "but it doesn't pay the grocer. There is very little work to be had locally. People are having to leave and move to a bigger city to get jobs."

"So?" Esmee demanded. "The point is that they can get jobs in the city and, when they do, we can keep the rural tone of our village."

No, Vicky thought. The point was that James, who had more of the world's goods than any person she had ever meet, was concerned about how normal, everyday people survived. Not only concerned about them, but was actively doing something to help.

Vicky stifled a sigh, wishing she knew more about James and Esmee's relationship. She could hardly ask James. She simply didn't have the kind of sangfroid necessary to carry off asking a question like, "So tell me, James, what is the relationship between you and your obnoxious neighbor? Are you romantically involved? Sleeping together?"

All the assertiveness training in the world would never get her to that point. Which left Sophie as her only source of information, and Sophie clearly loathed Esmee. Sophie wouldn't be likely to give Vicky an unbiased view.

"I don't want a company building here. And a foreign one at that." Esmee managed to invest the word *foreign* with all kinds of hidden meanings.

"Then it's a good thing nobody needs your permission, isn't it?" Sophie suggested.

"My uncle is on the planning committee," Esmee returned.

"It's been ten years since your uncle has been sober enough to—"

"This is an excellent roast, Aunt Sophie," James hurriedly interrupted.

Sophie shook her head at him. "I don't understand this younger generation. Always wanting to pretend they don't see what's right under their noses."

James grinned at his aunt. "It's called good manners, and you were the one who taught the concept to me."

Vicky's heart twisted at the thought of James as a small boy learning etiquette from Sophie. Although… why hadn't his parents taught him?

The real Ms. Lascoe had given Vicky a thumbnail sketch of James, which included the fact that his parents had died when he was at Cambridge. So they'd been around when he'd been growing up. What kind of parents had they been, Vicky wondered. Good ones who, for some reason, hadn't thought manners were important or bad ones who hadn't wanted to be bothered? And if they had been bad ones, did that mean that James didn't have a role model for his own parenting? If that were true, then could he be a good father to her children?

A frisson of worry trickled through her to be immediately absorbed by the memory of James's endearing expression as he'd so seriously dried Edmond after his bath. She didn't know whether James had had a proper role model for parenting or not, but one thing she was sure of. He loved the twins.

Maybe his lack of a parental role model was what made him so susceptible to Nanny's overbearing manner, Vicky suddenly realized.

But even if all that were true, how did it impact her goal of playing a significant role in the twins' lives?

Maybe she could convince James to let her have primary care of the twins while he learned to be a proper father? She, at least, knew exactly what was involved in being a good mother. Her own parents had been terrific role models. She had never, ever doubted that they loved her and were vitally interested in her life. There wasn't a single day that went by that she didn't miss them.

"Are you tired, Vicky?" James's question caught her off guard. She'd thought he was listening to Esmee's monologue.

"No, why?" she asked.

"Because for a second there you looked...sad," he said.

Vicky felt a flicker of unease at his accurate reading of her reaction to the memory of her parents. The man was far too observant for her comfort.

"And what would she have to be sad about?" Esmee demanded. "She's getting to visit a stately home like Thayer House."

James ignored Esmee and continued to study Vicky until her nerves felt stretched to the breaking point. She needed to tell him who she really was, she thought distractedly. The guilt of her deception was coloring her every reaction to him. Making her look for hidden meanings in everything he said.

"I think I'll skip dessert," James suddenly announced, catching Vicky by surprise. And Esmee, too, if the expression on her face was anything to go by.

"I have some calls that I need to make. Good night, Esmee."

Dropping his napkin beside his empty plate, James got to his feet and left the room.

Vicky watched him go, wishing she could go with him. Not even the thought of one of Cook's fabulous desserts was enough to compensate for having to put up with Esmee's interrogation. But she couldn't just leave Sophie to cope with Esmee's bitchiness alone. Sophie was an old woman. She deserved a little peace.

Ah, well, Vicky thought on an inward sigh, think of it as a chance to practice what you learned in assertiveness training class. James's household gave one far too many opportunities to practice.

The minute James was gone, Esmee said, "You may have James fooled for the moment, Miss Whoever-you-really-are, but I don't for a moment believe you are a relation. I intend to look into matters."

Vicky felt like the dramatically delivered announcement should have been accompanied by a clap of thunder at the very least. But underneath her sense of annoyance at the woman's officiousness was the very real fear that Esmee might somehow find out that Vicky wasn't really Ms. Lascoe.

But how could she? There really was a Ms. Lascoe and she really was about Vicky's age and general build. If Esmee went looking, all she was likely to discover was that Ms. Lascoe wasn't really related to the Thayer family, and James already knew that.

Surely Esmee couldn't find out that she was really Mrs. Sutton, could she?

Chapter Eight

Maybe a good book would take her mind off her difficulties and the people causing them, Vicky thought as she left the dining room after the seemingly interminable meal was finally over. Maybe she could find another Greek gem like the sixteenth-century volume on ethics James had shown her.

Strangely enough, the possibility, which a few weeks ago would have filled her with unrestrained delight, raised no more than a flicker of interest.

She sighed as she headed toward the library. The problem was that her mind kept straying from the books to the books' owner. James Thayer was infinitely more interesting than his possessions. She shivered slightly as she savored the memory of the grin he'd given her at dinner. *Interesting* didn't begin to describe James. *Intriguing* came a little closer. And *fascinating* even closer. A woman could spend a lifetime and never completely plumb the depths of his personality. But it sure would be fun to try.

"Vicky?" The hushed whisper sent a surge of heat through her as her body recognized and responded to James's voice a second before her mind did.

She looked around and discovered an eye peering out at her from the crack in the study door.

"James! You startled me."

"Lower your voice before you give me away. Is she gone?"

"Your aunt Sophie went to her room to rest. I think conversing with Miss Defoe wore her out."

"Fighting with her, you mean," he said dryly. "You'd think she'd learn at her age."

Learn what? Vicky wondered. That Esmee was in her nephew's life to stay? And, more horrifically, in Edmond's and Mary Rose's lives to stay? It didn't bear thinking about.

As Vicky watched, the door opened farther to reveal a tantalizing glimpse of James's body. He'd taken off the jacket of the impeccably tailored gray suit he'd been wearing at dinner and rolled up the sleeves of his white shirt. Her mouth dried as she studied the light golden hair on his deeply tanned forearms. She could see the muscles in his arm ripple as he pushed the door open wider, and her breath shortened as she remembered what it had felt like to have his arms around her. They had enclosed the two of them in a world of their own. A magical world she had never visited before. A world she had never even suspected existed. A world she wanted very much to explore in much greater depth.

"I wasn't wondering where my aunt was. I was referring to Esmee."

James cautiously stepped out of the study and peered down the hallway toward the dining room.

"She's gone home," Vicky told him, trying to analyze his tone of voice. He certainly didn't sound lovesick. He sounded…faintly harassed.

"Did you want to see her before she left?" Vicky probed.

"What I want isn't at issue," he said obscurely.

And what precisely did that mean? Vicky wondered. That he had wanted to see Esmee after dinner, but hadn't expected her to? But that didn't tally with his almost furtive air when he'd first peered out of his study.

"Where are you going?" he asked.

"To the library to find a good book to read."

"I'll come, too."

To her delight, he fell into step beside her.

"I left a Sotheby's catalog there. I want to get it."

"What kind of catalog?" she asked curiously. From the looks of this place, James could be supplying Sotheby's, not buying from them.

"They have a couple of maps coming up for auction that are reputed to be from the early thirteenth century." James automatically stepped around her and opened the library door.

His gesture gave her a feeling of being cherished, even though she knew it was silly to feel that way. She might be perfectly capable of opening her own doors, but it was still nice to be the recipient of small courtesies.

"May I see the catalog?" Vicky asked. She was curious about the maps, but even more so she wanted to keep James talking.

"Of course." He strode over to the library table beneath the center window, picked up a thick pamphlet and handed it to her.

"The maps are on page seventeen," he said.

Vicky obediently turned to page seventeen and whistled soundlessly when she saw the minimum opening bid listed beneath them. Collecting antique maps was not a hobby to be pursued by the faint of heart nor the thin of checkbook.

"They do look nice," James said, having misread her sound of shock.

"The price sure doesn't. Even in pounds that seems like an awful lot of money to pay for an old anything."

"How about a copy of one of Cicero's letters from the eleventh century?"

"That's different! Have they really got one for sale?" she asked eagerly.

James chuckled. The sound washed through her, making her feel as if something fantastic were about to happen.

"It always is different when it's your hobby being discussed. And no, they don't have one. I do. In the munitions room."

The maps had come from the munitions room, too, Vicky remembered.

"I'll show it to you sometime," he promised. "I keep it in a sealed case because of the deterioration of the paper. It's much too fragile to be touched."

"I'd be content just to look," Vicky assured him. "What exactly is a munitions room?"

"Originally it was where the family kept armaments. Today, it's where I keep things that need special handling. Or special guarding. The munitions room has the most up-to-date security system to be had."

"Did your first wife share your interest in collecting maps?" Vicky hoped the question didn't sound as baldly intrusive to him as it did to her. But she wanted to know. She had to know, she tried to rationalize her growing preoccupation with his first wife. Romayne might not be interested in the twins at the moment, but that was no guarantee that she wouldn't become maternal in the future. The thought of any child, let alone one of hers, trying to cope with both Esmee and Romayne was enough to keep her up nights.

"Romayne was only interested in collecting currency. Hard currency."

Vicky blinked at his razor-sharp tone. He sounded like a man who didn't have a single illusion left about his ex-wife. But then, appearances could be deceptive, as she well knew. Hadn't she played the part of Zane's loving wife for years? Even when she knew that her dreams of happily-ever-after would never be realized.

"But you did marry her," Vicky risked commenting. "You must have loved her."

James walked over to the window and stared out at the garden for a long moment before saying, "Yes, I married her and, yes, I loved her."

His admission tore through Vicky, leaving a wound that ached painfully. What did you expect? she demanded of herself. For him to say that he had never loved Romayne? That he'd married her because...

Because why, she wondered. Why had James fallen in love with Romayne? What had been the woman's appeal?

"Why?" she blurted out before she could think better of the question.

"Why did I marry her?" he repeated slowly. "For starters, she looked like the answer to every adolescent fantasy I'd ever had."

Vicky swallowed the bitter taste his words left in her mouth. Her slight figure would never appeal to a man's adolescent fantasies, let alone fulfill them. Why was so much of their culture based on dumb things that a person couldn't do anything about? One thing was certain, she thought in grim determination, she intended to make sure that Edmond didn't pick a wife with his hormones. She was going to make sure her children didn't suffer through bad marriages because no one ever told them the facts of love and marriage and how sex appeal could throw a monkey wrench into everything.

"But it was more than that," James continued. "It was what she represented."

Oh, yeah, and what was that? Vicky thought nastily. Great sex in-house?

"She talked about us being a family and having children."

His words caught her by surprise. Being part of a family was that important to James?

Uncertainly Vicky chewed her lower lip as she digested the implications of his words. If his desire to be part of a family had propelled him into marriage with the unsuitable Romayne, then that meant he was less likely to give her custody of the twins. At least, she very much feared that was what it meant.

"But I couldn't make the marriage work," he said, sounding intensely frustrated. "No matter how hard I tried, I couldn't find a way to do it!"

Vicky was caught between a desire to throw her arms around James in an attempt to erase the naked pain she could hear in his voice and an equal urge to run from the depth of anger she could hear darkening his voice.

She most emphatically didn't want to do anything to cause him to redirect that anger at her, but on the other hand she couldn't just ignore what he'd said. It was too important.

"One person can't make a marriage work," Vicky responded to his words and not to the emotion she could sense behind them. "Take it from one who's been there. Marriage is a chancy business. It takes two people committed to making it work, if it's to have any hope of success. One person, no matter how motivated, simply can't do it."

"Yes, but..."

"But what?" Vicky demanded. "But you are so much better than everyone else that you can do it on your own?"

"One person may not be able to make a marriage work, but one person's deficiencies can make it fail," he muttered.

"You mean like one of the partners being an alcoholic or an addict or an abuser?"

"Nothing so dramatic. I simply mean that if family dynamics are a learned response and one of the partners never learns it, then that partner dooms the marriage from the start."

"Not necessarily. My parents were married for over forty years, and they had a fantastic marriage. I learned what makes a marriage work very early, and it still wasn't enough."

"Enough for what?" James asked.

"It wasn't enough to allow me to make a success of my marriage. And believe me, I tried. My damnedest. Eventually I had to admit that marriage takes two people giving it their best shot or it's no go."

Two? James examined her words. Was it possible that the breakdown of his marriage wasn't entirely his fault? That it would have broken up even if he had come from a normal family and had had happy memories of his parents to draw on?

"How long did you try before you got divorced?" James asked.

Vicky opened her mouth to tell him that a divorce hadn't been necessary. Her husband's carelessness while driving a car at eighty miles an hour had made her a widow before she had a chance to become a divorcee. But then she remembered that she was supposed to be Ms. Lascoe.

Was this the time to come clean and tell him the truth? Nervously Vicky peered at him. His features were still tightly clenched with the strength of his feelings. She could almost see the powerful emotions swirling through his dark eyes. The anger he was bound to feel when she told him she'd lied to him would be added to the angry memories of his failed marriage. There was no telling how he'd react. He might focus all that anger on her. Which would doom any chance of talking about the twins' custody tonight. Maybe for weeks to come.

No, she finally decided. This was not the time to confess. She'd tell him later when he was calm.

But if she wasn't going to tell him the entire truth, then she could at least try not to add any more lies to the ones she'd already told him.

"Sometimes it felt like the marriage had lasted far too long, and other times I felt that if I could just hang on a bit longer, I could figure something out," she said.

"God, I know exactly what you mean," he muttered in heartfelt tones.

"My client's parents also provided her with a happy marriage as a role model to draw on," Vicky said, cautiously introducing the twins. "She'll be able to teach the children what is and isn't important in making a marriage work.

"Now, about the twins," Vicky hurriedly said, before he could say anything. "Since you actually have very little to do with the twins' care while they are babies…"

"I am with them full-time."

"No, Nanny is with them full-time. You see them once a day. Mrs. Sutton is a widow with no outside distractions. She is fully prepared to devote all her time to caring for them."

"I will not let the twins out of my house, let alone out of the country. I told you they are English."

"My client will formally agree that they are English. But English or American, they will be better off having a primary caregiver who is doing it because she loves them, not because it's her job to do it."

What would it be like to have someone taking care of you not because it was their job, but because they wanted to? Because they enjoyed spending time with you? James considered the radical idea.

He couldn't imagine. His own nanny had done a competent job. He'd always had meals on time, clean clothes, she'd even listened to his prayers at night, but he couldn't ever remember her putting her arms around him and hugging him just because she was glad he was there. It had been left to his aunt Sophie to do that on the occasions she had visited.

And now Vicky was claiming that her client was prepared to love his children. That Mrs. Sutton was willing to spend her time taking care of them. Not for monetary reward, but for…for what?

What did Mrs. Sutton expect to gain from taking care of the twins? The question nagged at him. No matter what Vicky claimed, in his experience, people, be they men or women, didn't do things for entirely altruistic reasons. They expected something in return. So what did the unknown Mrs. Sutton expect to get out of the situation?

She might have told Vicky that her only motivation was loving the twins, but that didn't make it true. Her motivation could be much more devious. She could be intending to use the children's social standing to ensure that she was able to move in the upper circles of English society. In fact, that would tally with her willingness to allow the twins to be English instead of American. On the other hand, her motives could be monetary despite the fact that his lawyer had said she had an easy competence. She could be expecting him to pick up her bills in exchange for caring for the children. Or she could have some entirely different motivation. The situation lent itself to endless possibilities. Vicky was simply too trusting when it came to Mrs. Sutton.

"Even if her motivation is as pure as you seem to think it is and all she wants to do is love my children—"

"She wants to love *her* children," Vicky inserted. "You are irrelevant from her point of view."

"How fortunate that biology doesn't agree with your client. But the point I am trying to make is that sooner or later she's going to remarry. They always do."

"She has a name, Mrs. Sutton. She isn't some generic they."

"Actually being a unique individual means that she is more likely to remarry," James insisted. "And if Edmond and Mary Rose are living with her, then they would be subjected to some unknown man's influence."

"She is a widow," Vicky said.

"Widows remarry all the time. Particularly since she has her parents' happy marriage to show her the advantages of being married."

"My client would be willing to agree not to remarry," Vicky said.

"You can't make promises like that for her. Hell, she can't make them for herself. They'd be unenforceable in law. And it's a moot point, anyway. All she'd have to do is to let the guy move in with her."

Vicky bit her lip in frustration. She wished she could tell him she wasn't making promises for a client. She was making them for herself. And they were promises she had no intention of breaking. She'd tried marriage, and it had been a disaster from start to finish. It wasn't a risk she was prepared to take again.

Although... Thoughtfully her eyes lingered on James's serious features. If she had been lucky enough or smart enough to have married a man like James Thayer, then maybe she would feel differently. He would certainly have been a unique husband. One who actually expected to put some effort into making his marriage work.

"My children will never live anywhere except under my roof," he stated flatly.

"Think about the children's needs," Vicky snapped. "You're all tied up in what you want. Try considering what they might want."

"They are too young to know what they want."

"Children need their mother. Do you think Edmond and Mary Rose are going to thank you if you make them the center of a nasty custody battle?"

"I won't be the one starting a custody battle," he

insisted. "I already have custody. It will be Mrs. Sutton who does it."

Vicky grimaced. "That is the most fallacious reasoning I have ever heard."

"It is not."

"Is, too," she retorted, and then paused as the sound of her voice filled her ears. "I can't believe that I have allowed myself to get suckered into such a childish argument."

"It isn't childish."

"It is when it descends to the level of 'is not, is, too,'" she said dryly.

"Does this mean you aren't going to argue with me anymore?" James asked.

"No. This means that I'm going to raise the intellectual level of the argument."

"Good luck. The whole problem with this thing is that it isn't intellectual. It's emotional. Your client wants my children."

"My client wants her children!" Vicky's voice rose with the strength of her frustration. "They aren't yours in a vacuum. They are both of yours, and the sooner you admit it the better."

"I have already admitted it," he insisted, "or I wouldn't have allowed you to come."

"I'm talking about admitting it emotionally, not intellectually."

James ran his long fingers through his hair in frustration. "I'm trying, dammit. But I'm not much good at emotional things."

"So, practice."

James stared at her, an arrested expression on his face.

Vicky felt a shiver of some errant emotion slither

through her at the gleam that suddenly sparked to life in his eyes.

"Practice?" he said.

"That's what I said," she repeated cautiously.

"Will you help me practice?" he asked.

Every instinct Vicky had went into overdrive at the devilment she could see in his face. What had happened? she wondered in confusion. One minute they'd been a step away from an all-out argument and the next minute he was...

Was what? she tried to figure it out. What was he thinking? Somehow, she didn't think it had to do with the twins.

"Sure I'll help you practice," she said, trying to sound more knowing than she felt.

"Good." He gave her a grin that ratcheted up the anticipation swirling through her. "I was hoping an intellect like you would be in favor of learning."

Intellect? Vicky's sense of frustration momentarily dampened her excitement. Why, just once in her life, couldn't a man look at her and see a sexually attractive woman? He didn't have to think she was some kind of sex goddess. She'd settle for being an attractive woman first and a smart woman second...just once. Her thoughts scattered into irretrievable fragments when James's arms unexpectedly closed around her.

Startled, she glanced up into his face, which was only inches from her own. She blinked uncertainly, trying to force her sluggish mind to think past the sensations pouring through her. Why had he taken her in his arms?

She stared at his mouth as she tried to figure it out, but all she could concentrate on were his lips. On their intriguing shape. On their firm texture. On the white gleam of his teeth as his mouth lifted in a smile that tightened the coil of excitement building in her.

She closed her eyes to shut out the tempting distraction and felt his arms tighten fractionally. He was so strong, she thought, as his arms gathered her closer to his chest. So very, very masculine.

His lips closed over hers, and she gave up all pretense of thinking. Feeling offered so many more possibilities. Feeling his lips pressing against hers, feeling his arms binding her against him, feeling the tingling sensation in her breasts as they were squashed against his hard chest.

Vicky shivered as his lips increased their pressure. Mindlessly she opened her mouth to his demands. His arms tightened convulsively and his tongue surged inside to taste her.

Vicky began to tremble, making her feel that the only thing keeping her on her feet was his grasp. That without the support of his arms she would simply slide to the floor and dissolve into a smoldering puddle of sensual desire.

A small moan of desire bubbled out of her throat as his tongue began to explore the warm cavern of her mouth. She wanted so much more.

Longingly she pressed closer. If only there weren't all these clothes between them, she thought in frustration. If only she could feel his skin against hers. If only she could run her hands over his bare chest. If only she could explore the tight muscles of his abdomen and then dip lower to...

A loud buzzing rang in her ears, rudely shattering her building euphoria. A haunting sense of loss filled her as his arms dropped, leaving her standing alone, feeling bereft.

She forced open her heavy eyelids and stared at James. His features seemed sharper somehow. Tighter. As if he had been as affected by what they had shared as she had been.

The possibility helped steady her.

"Turn it off," he said.

Would that she could, Vicky thought in confusion. In fact, she would have preferred to have never turned it on in the first place. Sexual awareness was not a comfortable thing to deal with. She quivered as an errant memory of the feel of his lips shot through her.

It... Her watch! The source of the noise suddenly penetrated. Her alarm was going off.

Hastily she took a step back and depressed the alarm function on her watch. It was easier to think with a little space between them. Not that she wanted to think about that kiss. It was filled with too many implications, all of which promised complications.

Nervously she stole a glance at James, trying to decide what to say that would convince him that... That what? she wondered. That she was so sophisticated that she kissed men like that all the time? Would it be better if he thought that? Or would it be better if he realized just how mind shattering she had found his kiss? She didn't have a clue.

"What did you set the alarm for?"

Vicky grabbed James's question like a lifeline. A safe, nonemotionally charged lifeline.

"To remind me to go up to the nursery and read the twins a bedtime story." She relaxed slightly when her voice came out sounding vaguely normal.

James looked into her delicate features and quashed an urge to kiss her again. Either that or swear. How could she look so serene and talk so calmly about reading a bedtime story when he felt as if someone had tightened every nerve ending in his body? Hadn't she felt even a fraction of what he had? What would it take to involve her fully in a kiss? He didn't know, but he was sure he wanted to explore the subject. In depth. But at least she hadn't slapped him for kissing her. The thought cheered him. Nor had she hit him with a bunch of questions about his motives. Questions that he couldn't answer because he didn't know. Somehow, around Vicky, he found himself doing all kinds of things he hadn't meant to do.

A tremor coursed through him at the memory of that kiss. And enjoying them, too.

He'd simply follow her lead, he decided. He might not like it that she was able to dismiss his lovemaking so easily, but it left him able to carry on as if nothing out of the ordinary had happened. And there was always tomorrow. His heartrate quickened.

"Why are you going to read them a story?" he asked as they walked to the nursery.

"One reads children bedtime stories." Vicky concentrated on regaining full control of her emotions before she reached the nursery. And Nanny's gimlet gaze.

"But why? The twins certainly can't understand them."

"A whole lot of reasons." Vicky earnestly quoted the childcare book. "First, it creates an emotional bond. Second, it creates pleasant memories for the child concerning books. Third, it helps the child's intellectual development."

"All that from reading a storybook?" James said skeptically.

"Absolutely," Vicky insisted as she pushed open the nursery door.

"Yes?" Nanny was sitting on the floor beside the twins who were lying on a blanket. Edmond was kicking his feet with great abandon while Mary Rose was watching him as if amazed by his performance.

"I've come to read a bedtime story to the twins," Vicky announced, bracing herself for an argument.

To her shock Nanny gave her an approving nod. "An excellent idea, Ms. Lascoe. There are several books in the bookcase there."

Nanny gestured toward a small, white, painted bookcase against the far wall. "I'll get their cribs ready." She went into the night nursery.

Vicky picked a book at random. What she read to them wasn't important. What was important was that she was reading to them.

Dropping down on the blanket beside the twins, she gathered Edmond in her arms. After a moment's hesitation James picked up Mary Rose and sat down beside her.

Vicky gulped as he inched closer, till she could feel his thigh pressed against hers and the hardness of his biceps against her arm.

"There," he muttered in satisfaction, when he was finally close enough to constrict her breathing. "Now Mary Rose can see the pictures, too."

"Good," Vicky said brightly and opened the book, carefully holding it out of reach of Edmund's clutching fingers.

Vicky looked over the short fable and said to James, "You can be the fox. I'll be the crow and the narrator."

"Me?"

"Sure, there are no passengers in parenting," she said.

"Let me guess," he muttered. "Your precious Mrs. Sutton plans to read them six books every day."

Vicky ignored his grumbles and started the story. When she got to the fox's first line, she paused, while he read it in a monotone.

"No, no," Vicky said. "You have to put feeling into it, James. Read it with meaning."

"There's plenty of meaning in my voice," he muttered. "It's called embarrassment."

Vicky giggled. "Embarrassment is a luxury no parent can afford. Just wait. They'll embarrass you on a weekly basis when they get older. Think back on a few of the things you did or said in public."

James did and felt a sense of sadness. He couldn't remember ever having been in public with his parents. Even on their semiannual visits they hadn't taken him anywhere.

"Now, once more from the top, with feeling," Vicky persisted.

"All right," James said. If this was going to give his own kids better memories of their childhood than he had, then he was willing to make a fool of himself.

Taking a deep breath, James launched into his best rendition of a smooth-talking con artist.

"Very good." Vicky gave him a warm smile of approval that he found almost as intoxicating as her kiss had been. Somehow, life seemed so full of fantastic possibilities when she was around.

And she was so loving toward the twins. James watched as she snuggled Edmond closer. Vicky would make a wonderful mother, and she clearly liked kids. So why hadn't she wanted any? Or hadn't her husband wanted them? Was it possible she might consider mothering some other woman's kids? A sudden excitement tore through him at the thought of her as the twins' mother. An excitement that reached fever pitch as he realized that in order for her to be the twins' mother she would first have to become his wife.

Chapter Nine

James grimaced in annoyance at his inability to keep his mind focused on the details of the financing plan he was drawing up for Herr Murchin. Despite the fact the plant meant a great deal to him, his thoughts kept straying to Vicky.

Maybe if he were to do nothing but think about her for the next five minutes, he could get her out of his system and get back to work, he decided.

Leaning back in his leather desk chair, he closed his eyes. His mind immediately produced an image of Vicky as she'd read the fable of the fox and crow for the twins. A glow of warmth sparked to life in his chest as he remembered the exact tilt of her lips as they'd curved in approval when he'd read the part of the fox. He hadn't felt as idiotic as he must have sounded. He'd felt rewarded. Ten feet tall as he'd basked in the glow of her encouraging smile.

And when Mary Rose had gurgled in delight at his mock growls, he'd felt euphoric. For a priceless moment, he'd not only felt as if he were part of a real family, he'd felt like a valued member of it. He'd wished with all his heart it were true.

"But wishes don't make reality," he muttered to himself.

He'd blown his chance to be part of a complete family.

Although... James frowned thoughtfully as he remembered what Vicky had said about one person not being able to make a marriage work. That it took two. If she were right...

Did that mean there was a chance he could make a success of a second marriage if he could find someone who was willing to work at it with him? But it couldn't just be anyone. It had to be someone who was willing to include the twins in the relationship. Someone who would love them wholeheartedly. Someone who was willing to be a mother to them.

James's features softened as he remembered the tender expression on Vicky's face as she had cuddled Edmond in her arms. The way she had dropped an approving kiss on his small head when he'd babbled along with her reading.

It was odd that she could be so sexually attractive and yet be so maternal at the same time. He didn't understand it, but it was undeniably true.

And Vicky knew all about being trapped in a bad marriage. He remembered the pain in her voice when she'd talked about her ex. She knew that building a successful marriage took a great deal of effort.

But just because she knew what needed to be done didn't mean that she was willing to try a second marriage. Particularly not with a man who had the added complication of two children. But she liked Mary Rose and Edmond, he argued with himself. There was no way she could fake the pleasure in her face when she held them. Nor any reason for her to try.

But there was another complication, he conceded. The twins' bio-mother, Mrs. Sutton. Vicky's client. Although maybe Mrs. Sutton wouldn't be as serious a problem as he'd originally thought. She was Vicky's relative, and, if she were anything like Vicky, it was possible she could be a good influence on the twins. Vicky certainly felt she would be, and Vicky's judgments had been accurate so far. Maybe he should allow Mrs. Sutton to visit so he could judge what she was like for himself.

As for Vicky...he'd do everything he could to encourage the growth of their relationship without making her feel pressured, he decided. And he could start his campaign this afternoon at the auction at Beddlington Manor.

A feeling of intense anticipation gripped him as he checked the time. Another hour and fourteen minutes before they left—before he could get Vicky away from all the distractions at Thayer House. With a little luck, he might even be able to get her alone long enough to kiss her. His heart began to beat in slow heavy thumps.

He grimaced. Hell, he didn't want to kiss her. Kissing her was like throwing a starving man a few crumbs. He wanted to make love to her. Again and again.

Don't rush things, he counseled himself. Take it slow and easy or you risk losing everything.

Determinedly he turned back to the proposal he'd been trying to work on.

Vicky watched as James handed his auction invitation through the car window to the burly man at the end of the driveway.

"Good afternoon, Mr. Thayer." The man's voice

was respectful, although his eyes were watchful as they studied Vicky.

"Ms. Lascoe is with me," James said as Vicky froze in absolute panic. What would she do if the man demanded identification? Nervously her eyes flicked to the purse in her lap. Inside was a wallet full of ID. Identification for Vicky Sutton, aka Mrs. Zane Sutton, not for Vicky Lascoe.

Vicky swallowed against her stomach's sudden nervous churning. Of all the ways she had anticipated telling James she wasn't really Ms. Lascoe, being caught out by a security man hadn't even crossed her mind.

"Ms. Lascoe isn't on the list," the man said uncertainly.

Vicky frantically searched her skittering thoughts for inspiration and came up blank. She should have realized that security would be tight considering the value of some of the items being sold.

"Ms. Lascoe is my house guest," James said patiently. "She is also a family connection."

"If you'll vouch for her, Mr. Thayer," the man finally said.

"Certainly I will," James said.

"You can leave your car here, sir," the man said. "Someone will park it for you."

Vicky hastily scrambled out of the Mercedes, wanting to escape before the man changed his mind.

She didn't feel easier until they had rounded the corner of the hedges and were out of sight.

"I'm not used to security at auctions," she said, offering an explanation in case James had noticed her tenseness.

"There are some very valuable things being offered today," James said. "Derwood was an eclectic collec-

tor, but he specialized in the French Impressionists. He
has several museum-quality Monets."

"I'm surprised they would sell them here," Vicky
said with a curious look at the rigid formality of the
extensive grounds. The house wasn't anywhere near as
inviting as Thayer House even if it did appear to be as
well cared for.

"Serious art collectors tend to prefer privacy,"
James told her. "And it's harder for art thieves to hide
themselves in the country."

"Where are the maps you want to bid on?" Vicky
glanced furtively around the baronial entrance hall as
they entered, afraid of finding another, more thorough,
security man.

"I didn't mean to worry you about art thieves."
James noticed her look. "Peveneces of London is handling the security, and they're very good."

Vicky gave him a weak smile, resisting the impulse
to tell him that Peveneces weren't nearly as good as he
thought.

James checked the catalogue he was holding, and
said, "The maps are in the upstairs gallery. There's
also some Roman statuary in the conservatory. Would
you like to take a look at it?"

Vicky briefly considered the pleasure of looking at
some of her beloved Roman remains, weighed it
against the pleasure of watching James's expressive
features as he studied his Medieval maps and jettisoned
Rome without a second thought.

"Maybe we can check out the statues later if there's
time," she said. "First, let's go look at the maps."

James rewarded her choice with a smile that sent
shivers of longing over her skin. She wanted to throw
herself into his arms and kiss him and to heck with the

auction. Later, she promised herself. Later, she would try to figure out a way to get close to him.

They quickly located the maps hanging on a wall by themselves. There was no one else around.

"Does this mean you have no competition for them?" Vicky asked curiously.

"I doubt it. Anyone seriously interested in them would have had them authenticated earlier. They really are magnificent," James said appreciatively.

Vicky watched James as he studied the delicate maps. His face was alight with an eager fascination that made him seem younger somehow. Younger and more approachable.

"It gives me an odd feeling," he said, "to think of someone making those maps over eight hundred years ago."

"It gives me an even odder feeling to think of the explorer who brought back the information so some cartographer could draw it," Vicky said.

"Exploring was a dangerous occupation. But what the man learned survived him by centuries."

"And we can be sure he was a man," Vicky sniped. "The powers that were would never have let a woman go exploring."

James chuckled at her indignant expression. "Be that as it may, the women of the time did leave evidence of their passing. I'll show you the tapestries they have for sale. They're from about the same era, and they were woven by the stay-at-home wives."

James took her arm in what appeared to be nothing more than his normal good manners. Vicky found his touch anything but causal. The hard warmth of his fingers seemed to burn through the thin blue linen of her suit jacket. Her skin absorbed the heat, sent it racing along her nerve endings and allowed it to dislodge all kinds of inconvenient longings.

She wanted to caress the back of his hand. She wanted to push her fingers beneath his gray suit jacket and rub over the light brown hair that covered his muscular forearms. She wanted to probe his muscles and learn their exact definition. And those weren't the only muscles she wanted to explore.

Vicky stole a quick sideways glance at his wide chest. She'd bet he looked pretty spectacular without his shirt. Her mouth dried at the thought. Would the same brown hair that decorated his arms cover his chest? Her palms began to tingle as she contemplated running her hands over his chest.

Down, girl, Vicky told herself. She had about as much chance of getting him out of his clothes and into some serious lovemaking as she did of getting him to sign over custody of the twins. Zero-to-none. The fact that he had kissed her didn't mean a thing in the sophisticated circles James Thayer moved in. So try to respond with a little sophistication yourself, she told herself.

The problem was, she thought with an inward sigh, that she *wasn't* sophisticated. Not even a little bit.

The reminder of just how different she was from this cosmopolitan man vaguely depressed her, but she refused to dwell on their differences. They had a lot in common, too, she assured herself. Both had survived bad marriages. Both of them had absorbing hobbies that neatly dovetailed. And she was sure that, given the chance, she would find his house as interesting as he did. There was so much fascinating history connected to it. Real personal history about real people, who were James's relatives. But their strongest bond was the children they shared. They both thought Mary Rose and Edmond were the most fantastic babies ever born.

"The tapestries are through here in the long refractory." James gestured toward an oddly shaped wooden door that curved at the top of the arch to a point. It was made of some very dark wood and couldn't have been more than six feet tall.

"These old houses make one aware of just how stunted previous generations must have been without all our vitamins and nutrition," Vicky said as she went through the small door, instinctively ducking her head.

James followed her into a long, narrow room.

Hanging from wooden frames in the middle of the room were half a dozen tapestries of various sizes.

"Please do not touch the tapestries," a bored-looking guard by the door rattled off. "The fabric is extremely fragile and the oils from people's fingers cause irreparable damage," the guard finished and then gave them a glare as if daring them to dispute his words.

"I wouldn't dream of touching anything that old," Vicky said soothingly.

"That makes you unique in this crowd, miss. And would you believe, most of them are representatives from museums!" The guard shook his head in disgust.

"Shocking," Vicky sympathized.

The man gave her an approving nod and went back to the book he'd been reading.

Vicky wandered over to the tapestry, followed by James. She leaned closer, studying the intricate weaving.

"The amount of work that must have gone into this boggles the mind," she said.

"What else did they have to do with their time?"

James said. "Their men were off fighting someone or other, their children were cared for by the servants."

"The English aristocracy seems to have a long tradition of leaving their children in the care of hirelings. Maybe if those women had spent more time shaping their sons' moral values, their daughters-in-law would have had husbands content to stay at home instead of being out harrying their poor neighbors!"

"That's a simplistic view of both history and human nature," James countered.

"Maybe, but it's still going on. Your children are being cared for by a hireling."

"That is hardly the same thing." James defended himself as he followed her around the back of the largest of the tapestries. "I don't have a wife to care for my children."

"The children have a mother who is quite willing to do it," Vicky reminded him. "You chose to be obstructive about it."

"I am not being obstructive! I don't know that Mrs. Sutton would be good for the twins."

"And you think Attila the Nanny is? Talk about arbitrary! To say nothing of irrational. Tell me, if you refuse to meet the twins' mother, how are you ever going to find out what she is like?"

James frowned slightly, remembering his earlier thoughts on having Mrs. Sutton visit. Maybe it was time…

James sent up a muddled prayer that he was doing the right thing and said, "All right, she can come."

"What?" Vicky jerked around and stared at him in shock.

"I said, your precious Mrs. Sutton can visit the twins. There's a cottage she can use out behind the glasshouses. I had it restored for a retired employee who has since gone to live with her daughter in the south of Spain. It's been sitting empty since.''

It sounded perfect, Vicky thought happily. She would be able to see the twins in the relative privacy of a separate dwelling. She could have them all to herself. She could learn how to be a mother without having Nanny standing over her correcting her efforts.

But James thought Mrs. Sutton was someone else entirely. What was he going to say when she told him who she really was?

She stole a quick glance at him to find him studying her with an earnest expression that tore at her heart and increased her sense of guilt to suffocating levels.

Would his offer still be open when she told him who she really was? Or would he withdraw it and tell her to get out? Damn, she thought in discouragement. She wished she hadn't lied to him in the beginning, but if she hadn't lied to him then, she wouldn't be here now. Her lawyer would have come in her place, and who knew how that might have turned out. Ms. Lascoe hadn't been eager to come to England. She hadn't wanted to leave either her fiancé or her busy practice.

Her grandmother had been right, Vicky conceded with hindsight. Deceiving people really did lead to a very tangled web. She just hoped that in her efforts to untangle this particular web she didn't irreparably break something. Such as James's sudden desire to compromise.

She had to tell him the truth. But not now. Not at a public auction that he had been looking forward to. He wanted to bid on those maps. He didn't need the distraction of finding out who she really was. She'd tell him later. Tonight after the twins' good-night story. This time she wouldn't wimp out.

''Thank you for the generous offer,'' Vicky murmured into the silence, which, her screaming nerves told her, had gone on far too long.

"You're welcome," James said, confused by her reaction to his offer. She should have been ecstatic at the news that she'd been successful. That he was going to allow her client access to his children. So why wasn't she?

He studied the finely drawn tension in her face. Not only did she not look happy, she looked…upset, he finally decided. But that made no sense. Why would she be upset? Unless…

A sudden surge of excitement coursed through him. Could Vicky be upset because she realized that having gotten his consent for her client to come, her job was done? Could she like him well enough to want to stay in his home a little while longer? It was an intoxicating idea. But how could he test his theory?

He glanced around the room. It was still deserted except for the guard at the door who was deep in a rather lurid-looking detective novel.

"There's a much smaller tapestry I wanted to check out," James said, hoping the uncertainty he was feeling wasn't apparent in his voice. "It should be behind these big ones."

He gestured to his left.

To his satisfaction, Vicky moved behind the large hanging out of sight of the guard.

"It must be back here." James led her deeper into the labyrinth of hangings, mentally thanking whoever had hung them.

They rounded the corner of a large tapestry depicting a battle to find a small hanging, about three-feet-by-four. It depicted a unicorn sitting in a field of multi-colored flowers. There was a small blond girl with a chain of some bluish flowers in her hair leaning against the unicorn.

Vicky's breath caught in her throat at the exquisite beauty of it. "It's gorgeous," she breathed reverently.

"Yes, gorgeous."

The odd note in James's voice caught her attention, and she turned to find him staring not at the tapestry but at her. Surely he didn't mean that she was gorgeous, did he? She dismissed the attractive idea the second after it occurred to her. This was James Thayer. A wealthy, sophisticated aristocrat. He not only knew what real feminine beauty was, he'd been married to a prime example of it.

"The girl in the tapestry reminds me a little of Mary Rose." Vicky forced her attention back to the tapestry. "She has the same blond hair and sweet expression."

"Yes," James agreed, still without looking at the hanging.

Vicky nervously ran her tongue over her lower lip, watching uncertainly as his eyes followed the movement. Could his interest really be in her? Had he brought her back here to see the hanging or had he brought her back here to kiss her? That was the question. If he didn't want to kiss her, and she encouraged him...

What? She scoffed at her fears. The sky will fall? The world will stop? Hardly. He'd simply ignore her invitation and they'd go back to the auction. And she'd be embarrassed out of her mind, she conceded.

But if she encouraged him and he kissed her, she'd be floating back to the auction on a euphoric cloud. The rewards of getting to kiss him were well worth the risks of being rebuffed. She hoped.

Taking heart from the gleam she could see in his eyes, she inched slightly closer to him.

"I think…" Her voice trailed away as the scent of his cologne drifted to her.

"I'm not," he muttered.

"Not what?"

"Thinking. I'm too busy feeling, and wishing I could feel more."

"Really?" she muttered.

It was all the encouragement he needed. His arms closed around her with satisfying eagerness, and he pulled her up against his chest. His mouth swooped down, and he captured her lips as if starved for the taste of her. It was a sentiment Vicky heartily agreed with. Without reservation, she opened her mouth to the pressure of his lips and was rewarded when his tongue slipped inside.

Reaction poured through her, making her feel weak and light-headed. As if he understood, his arms tightened, holding her steady against him as his mouth continued to plunder the essence of hers.

"Hurry up, Henry. The auction is about to start, and I need to check the back of this big one for moth holes."

Henry? The faintly nasal voice punctured Vicky's sense of rightness. Henry didn't belong in her dreams. Or as a witness to her kiss.

"If you would just once stop and ask for directions instead of wandering around claiming you know where you are, we wouldn't be this late. And Father is going to be so upset," the whiny voice continued.

"Let's hope Father, whoever he is, does the pair of them in," James muttered against her softly swollen lips.

The fact that James sounded as upset as she was by the interruption cheered her a little, and she was able to accept his withdrawal from her without grabbing for him.

"It's right behind—" The woman's voice broke off as she rounded the corner and saw them.

"Oh, dear," she said with an archness that set Vicky's teeth on edge. "Have we interrupted something?"

"Not at all," James said politely.

Vicky watched in fascination as James turned slightly and the woman got a good look at him. Her expression changed from smug to shock to an eagerness to please in the space of seconds.

"Why, Mr. Thayer, I didn't know it was you back here with…" She stared at Vicky in open curiosity.

"How could you?" James replied and, taking Vicky's arm, escorted her out of the room.

"Who was that woman?" Vicky asked once they were safely seated in the auction.

"I haven't a clue, nor do I wish to find out," James said.

"But she recognized you," Vicky persisted.

"She recognized the owner of Thayer House," James corrected her. "She doesn't know me."

Maybe not, but Vicky would have been willing to bet that the cupidity she'd seen in the woman's eyes had been for James, the man, and not James, the owner of Thayer House. James seemed to be oblivious to the effect he had on women in general and her in particular. Was it because his first wife had treated him as nothing more than a means to an end?

"Whatever you do, don't make any sudden movements or sounds once the auction begins." James's instructions broke into her thoughts.

"I thought all those stories about people accidentally buying things at auctions were just that, stories."

"Yes and no. Since you didn't register beforehand, they wouldn't try to make you honor anything you accidentally bid on, but a false bid would really annoy the auctioneer, to say nothing of our fellow buyers."

Vicky glanced curiously around at the chairs full of people. They were a very diverse lot, ranging from fashionably dressed jet-setters to professional types who were probably the museum experts the guard had been so scathing about.

"An eclectic collection of people."

"This kind of affair usually is. Most of the people here are agents for various collectors or museums. They aren't buying for themselves. Although Wilton over there is." James gestured toward a stick-thin, elderly man sitting in the front row.

"He collects Georgian silver, and there were several good pieces listed in the catalog."

Vicky felt faintly depressed. James knew people who collected Georgian silver, and she knew people who collected things like ceramic pigs, souvenir teaspoons and hotel matchbook covers. But their differences didn't matter, she told herself. What mattered was their similarities, and there were lots of them. She just hoped there were enough of them to temper his reaction when she told him the truth tonight.

Chapter Ten

"A most successful afternoon," James announced with satisfaction as he pulled up in front of Thayer house and cut the Mercedes's engine.

If success was measured in terms of money spent, then the day had been a roaring success, Vicky thought with a nervous glance at the two antique maps and the exquisite unicorn tapestry James had so casually draped across the back seat. She had never, ever seen so much money change hands so quickly as she had at the auction. The memory still made her feel slightly faint.

On the other hand, if she measured the afternoon's success in terms of her own personal satisfaction it was an afternoon without parallel. Vicky studied James from beneath her eyelashes as she got out of the car. Not only did she have the memory of that stolen kiss behind the tapestries to cherish, but the rest of the afternoon, the part that had nothing to do with her compulsive sexual fascination with James had been equally memorable. She had quite simply had fun with him.

James Thayer had been full of dry wit, which he'd whispered in asides to her, making it very difficult for her to keep a straight face at times. A pleasurable sense of companionship filled her at the memory. She had felt as if she and James were a couple, a unit who shared the same ideas and goals. It was a feeling she'd never had before, she realized, as she carefully accepted the tapestry he handed her.

Not that she hadn't been physically attracted to men before. She had. But not anywhere near as deeply, as fundamentally as she was attracted to James. And she'd known other men who were fun to be around, but never before had she found one man who appealed to her both mentally and physically as James did. And that didn't even take into account her feelings about the fact that he was the father of her children.

Her reaction to him was so odd. It was…

A chill feeling of panic feathered over her skin, tightening the muscles of her stomach and giving her the unsettling feeling that she'd just stepped off a step that wasn't there. It wasn't odd, she realized with dawning horror. It was a disaster. And it was a disaster because she was *in love* with the man.

Vicky briefly closed her eyes, willing the unwelcome bit of self-revelation not to be true. She didn't want to be in love with James Thayer. She simply couldn't be. She could like him. Liking him was all right. In fact, liking was good. She was going to be seeing James on a regular basis because of the children. Liking him would make the contact easier.

But loving him would complicate her life beyond belief. How could she possibly keep her emotions under wraps every time she had to talk to him? She had no idea. All she knew was that she was going to have to figure it out. To let him find out that she had been so monumentally stupid as to fall in love with him was unthinkable. It would put her in the same category as some love-struck adolescent, without even the saving grace of being young. She couldn't bear for James to pity her. Even anger would be better than pity.

My God, she thought in despair, how had she managed to mess up her life to such an extent in such a short time? Surely a screwup of this magnitude should take weeks to accomplish, not mere days.

"Don't look so worried." James misunderstood the cause of her slightly frantic expression. "You aren't going to damage that tapestry. It's survived almost a thousand years. It isn't going to be hurt by you carrying it into the house."

Vicky made an effort to quash her growing panic. She'd worry later about all the problems loving James Thayer would cause. Right now she wanted to savor each and every moment with him before she was forced to tell him the truth.

"Why did you buy it?" Vicky nodded with her chin toward the tapestry. "I didn't think you were interested."

Oh, he was interested all right, James thought ruefully as his eyes lingered on the flush that tinted her soft cheeks. But it wasn't the tapestry that interested him, it was the person who had looked at it and seen a resemblance to his daughter. It was the person he'd kissed beside it. He hadn't bought the thing for himself. He'd bought it for Vicky. Because she'd admired it. But he could hardly tell her that. She might think he was trying to bribe her with an expensive gift.

Damn! he thought in frustration. Why couldn't he have met Vicky Lascoe without the problem of the twins' custody between them? Her representing Mrs. Sutton was causing all kinds of complications. He encouraged himself with the thought that they were not insurmountable ones.

"It was your comment about the little girl in the tapestry reminding me of Mary Rose. I thought she might like it when she gets older, and if she doesn't it will make a good addition to the collection here at Thayer House."

"It would make a good addition to the collection at the Louvre," Vicky said dryly.

"Good afternoon, Ms. Lascoe, sir." Beech appeared as if by magic, and James handed him the package containing the maps.

"Good afternoon, Beech. Put these maps in the munitions room, please. We'll keep Ms. Lascoe's tapestry for the moment. I want to show it to my aunt."

"The Lady Sophie?"

James glanced at Beech, his attention caught by the odd note in the butler's voice. He recognized the tone. Beech was stalling.

"I only have one aunt. Where is she?"

"She went to her meeting of the Women's Institute down in the village. And she refused to wait until I could find someone to drive her," he added in a rush. "She said she wanted to walk and commune with nature."

"Sounds like a harmless enough pleasure," Vicky said in defense of the old woman. It was nice that James loved his aunt, but he really needed to give her a little breathing space. He couldn't wrap her up in cotton wool and put her on a shelf to keep her safe.

"It isn't the walking, Ms. Lascoe." Beech gave her a troubled look. "It's…"

"Dammit to hell!" James bit out. "Don't tell me she was wearing her usual collection?"

"Yes," Beech muttered miserably.

All Vicky could think of was a line from an old television show in which the hero was always asking a question and then saying, "I told you not to tell me that."

She firmly pressed her lips together to hold back the giggle that threatened to escape. She very much doubted James would see the humor of the situation.

"How long ago did she leave?" James snapped.

"About an hour ago, sir. I tried to follow her, but my hip seized up, and today is Daniel's day off and the gardeners were nowhere to be found."

"It isn't your fault, Beech." James clamped down on his fear long enough to reassure the butler. "I'll go get her."

Without another word James turned on his heel and left the house at a brisk walk.

"Here, put this with the maps." Vicky hastily shoved the tapestry at Beech and sprinted after James. Somehow she had to make him see that he was wrong. That it didn't matter what anyone thought of Sophie's fashion sense or lack thereof. What mattered was that wearing all that costume jewelry made her feel good. And anything that made one feel good and wasn't illegal or immoral should be encouraged.

Vicky caught up with him at the edge of the porch and then lengthened her stride to match his longer legs.

"James, you're overreacting."

"Like hell I am!"

"What difference does it really make if your aunt likes to wear so much jewelry." She tried to reason with him. "It's a harmless enough idiosyncrasy."

"My aunt is not the only idiot!" He glared at Vicky. "One has to wonder what world you live in."

Vicky could feel the blood drain out of her face. She wanted to turn around and run back to the house. Away from his anger.

Running didn't work. She forced her shaking legs to keep moving. Five years of marriage to Zane had proved to her beyond a shadow of a doubt that problems didn't go away; they simply got bigger.

Facing an unreasonable attitude was the only way to deal with it. And she could do it, she encouraged herself. She'd faced down Nanny, hadn't she?

Vicky studied the clenched muscles along his jaw and barely suppressed a shudder. Nanny was not and never would be a match for James when it came to being formidable. But she'd dealt with him before, she reminded herself. She hadn't taken no for an answer when he'd tried to block her from seeing her children. And she had forced him to negotiate, even if she hadn't been able to force him to agree to her terms. At least she had made him compromise. Something she didn't think he did very often. She could deal with his anger. All she had to do was remember what she had learned in her assertiveness training class.

Vicky hurriedly searched through her churning thoughts, seeking enlightenment. The only thing she could clearly remember was an admonition not to allow oneself to be sucked into fights. To always keep the focus of the discussion on the concrete issue at hand.

"It's not important if people think your aunt's propensity for wearing a lot of jewelry is in bad taste," she said. "People who matter will simply view it as a harmless eccentricity."

James came to sudden halt, and Vicky unexpectedly

ran into him. She bounced slightly when her body collided against his. Frantically she struggled to force her already muddled thoughts past their unfortunate tendency to want to cling to him.

Words, she reminded herself. First, you must deal with the words. That's what relationships are built on. Words. Because without mutual understanding and respect, eventually even the strongest sexual attraction would consume itself and leave nothing. It took communication to provide an endless source of fuel to sustain a relationship. And she wanted to ground their relationship, whatever it was, on a solid foundation. Even if nothing could ever come of her love for James, there were still the children to think of.

"You think I give a damn what anyone thinks about what my aunt chooses to wear?" he demanded.

"If you don't care what anyone thinks, you're giving a great imitation of it," she said tartly. "Forbidding her to go out in public wearing all that costume jewelry."

"It isn't costume jewelry," he said succinctly.

"Isn't..." Vicky stared at him in disbelief. "But it has to be. Some of those rings are huge. That one dinner ring with the zircon she always wears must be... twenty-five carats."

"Thirty-two, and it's a diamond. A flawless, blue diamond. Cecil Rhodes gave it to my great-great grandmother. A lot of the rest of that stuff was made from stones brought back from India, starting with the Thayer who went out there in the late 1700s."

"That means your aunt is wearing..." Vicky gulped, unable to even guess at the monetary value of Sophie's accessories.

"I believe the expression is 'a king's ransom,'" James said dryly.

"Then why didn't you tell me?" Vicky demanded, hurrying after him as he started off toward the village again. "If you had just explained that they were real..." Vicky shuddered at the thought of the wealth all that jewelry represented and, even worse, what some people would do to get their hands on it.

"I told you she wasn't to wear them outside," he defended himself.

"I spent my entire married life being given orders without explanations," Vicky shot back. "I vowed I wasn't ever going to say 'yes and amen' to anyone's arbitrary orders again just to keep the peace. The emotional price was far too high. You should have explained the reason for your order to me."

Explained? James considered. Explaining wasn't something he did very often. His aunt went her own way no matter what rationale he presented to her. And his ex-wife had never really listened to him. Romayne had only paid attention to his words when they threatened something she wanted. Like when he'd finally had enough of their farce of a marriage and had demanded a divorce. Then she'd listened.

But if explaining made Vicky happy, then he was willing to give it a shot.

"I guess I should have explained," he offered.

"And I should have asked you why you didn't want her to wear it, instead of jumping to conclusions," Vicky admitted.

James blinked, taken aback by her willingness to accept part of the blame. His ex-wife had never, ever, accepted responsibility for what she'd done. Even when one of the scandal sheets had caught her in bed

with a married member of Parliament, she'd blamed
the reporter for the ensuing scandal. To find a woman
who was willing to accept responsibility for her actions
was as unexpected as it was novel.

"It was my course, you see." Vicky tried to explain
as she hurried along beside him. "I'm having some
trouble implementing it."

"What course?" James asked, curious about the way
her mind worked. For such an intelligent woman, her
thought processes sometimes seemed totally incompre-
hensible to him.

"The assertiveness training course I took. I realized
after my marriage failed that my husband couldn't have
run roughshod over me if I hadn't let him do it. The
problem was, I wasn't sure how to stop someone from
doing it again. So I took this course on how to assert
yourself, and it was full of great ideas. It's just that I
can't always figure out when I should be using the
technique and when I shouldn't."

"Assertiveness training?"

James studied her earnest features and felt an unexpected and totally uncharacteristic desire to pulverize
her ex-husband. If James had been lucky enough to
have found a woman like Vicky to love, he would have
cherished her, not browbeaten her. But at least the bas-
tard was an ex.

"It's a good thing you aren't a trial lawyer," he said.
"Lack of assertiveness would be a real problem in the
courtroom."

"Um, yes," Vicky muttered, having momentarily
forgotten that she was supposed to be Ms. Lascoe, who
from what Vicky had seen, could give the course's instructor a few tips on assertiveness. The sooner she got
up her courage and confessed, the better it would be.

It took too much energy to maintain the lies she'd told. She'd much rather expend that energy elsewhere.

She studied James out of the corner of her eye, her gaze lingering on the broad width of his shoulders beneath his gray suit jacket. The possibilities for expending energy with James were endlessly intriguing.

Vicky gave up trying to catalogue those possibilities when they reached the tiny village and James stopped in front of a long, redbrick building.

She watched as James scanned the area. Looking for anything out of the ordinary, Vicky assumed. There didn't appear to be anything to find. The building dozed in the late-afternoon sun. The only noise was the faint buzzing of a bee sampling the flower bed to the right of the door. The whole scene seemed to be straight out of a Constable painting labeled *Peaceful Summer Afternoon in Olde Rural England.*

James must have thought so, too, Vicky realized, because she could almost see the tension draining out of him.

"Now what do we do?" Vicky asked.

James felt a surge of some elusive emotion at Vicky's words. What do *we* do, she'd said. As if they were a team. As if they were in this together. For the second time since she'd come, he felt a sense of belonging. It might not be a rational reaction to her simple statement, but that was how he felt. As if he finally belonged.

With an effort, he shook off his own feelings in order to focus on his aunt's safety.

"We get Aunt Sophie out of there and home, where she'll be safe," he said.

"Good. I like a concise mission statement." Vicky gave him a grin, feeling much more cheerful now that she realized her encouragement of Sophie's desire to wear jewelry wasn't going to have any nasty repercussions.

"The best kind." James grinned back at her, warmed by her humor. It really was a wonderful day. First, he'd been able to see the twins in the morning thanks to Vicky's interference with Nanny's schedule, then he'd had hours at the auction to enjoy Vicky's company, and now she had, somehow, reduced his fear for his aunt's safety by sharing it. Vicky Lascoe was quite a woman. He just wished she was his woman.

Vicky followed James inside and down the hall toward the sound of women's voices.

James walked through the open door into a small room with Vicky hard on his heels. About forty women, ranging in age from younger than Vicky to older than Sophie, were seated on metal folding chairs in front of a long, brown table. Behind the table sat an overweight woman of about sixty who was wearing the most incredible purple hat. To her right a thin, middle-aged woman was industriously scribbling in a notebook. The president and the secretary, Vicky mentally labeled them.

As Vicky watched, the woman in the purple hat looked up and caught sight of James. Her mouth dropped slightly, and she stared at him as if shocked.

Vicky ignored an impulse to check to make sure that his fly wasn't open. Surely the sight of one lone man wasn't worthy of that much consternation.

Noticing their leader's reaction, the audience seemed to turn as one to see what she was looking at.

A young woman who had been loudly proclaiming the virtues of having a bottle booth—whatever that was—stopped in midharangue. The room went absolutely still.

Vicky automatically checked behind her to make sure a monster hadn't snuck up behind them to produce such an effect on the audience. The space was empty.

"Why, Mr. Thayer, sir." The purple-hatted lady jumped to her feet. "Whatever are you doing here?"

"James," Aunt Sophie greeted him from the first row. "What are you doing here?"

"We came to walk you home," James said calmly. None of his relief at seeing his beloved aunt unharmed was evident in his voice.

"Might as well. At the rate this argument is going on, the meeting will last all night.

"Have you ever noticed," she said as she got to her feet, "that the people with the most grandiose ideas are never there when it comes time to implement them. They leave all the work to others."

"I'll say," someone from the middle section muttered with a sideways glance at the red-faced woman who'd been arguing for the bottle booth when they'd come in.

"Goodbye, all." Sophie smiled benignly at her fellow committee members.

"Goodbye, Lady Sophie," they responded like a well-rehearsed Greek chorus.

"You didn't have to come after me," Sophie said, once they were outside away from the curious gazes. "It's only a step to the house."

"Oh, yes, we did," Vicky said, wanting to repair the damage her meddling had caused. "Sophie, when I told you should wear all that—" she waved at the collection Sophie was wearing, still finding it hard to believe that stones that big could be authentic "—stuff, I didn't know it was real."

"Not real?" Sophie blinked in confusion. "But why would you think the Thayer family collection would be fake? Unlike a lot of the old families, the Thayers have always been very astute businessmen. In fact, I doubt Henry, that was James's father, you know, ever gave more than passing notice to anything that didn't promise to return a profit in short order."

James's features tightened, and Vicky realized that Henry hadn't made an exception for his son.

"In retrospect, I should have," Vicky conceded, "but that's irrelevant. The fact is that if you wander around wearing a fortune in jewels, some criminal is likely to clobber you and take them."

"Around here?" Sophie asked skeptically with a wave of her thin, blue-veined hand at the bucolic countryside.

"The habitant of the criminal element is universal," Vicky insisted. "Not only do you cause James a great deal of worry when you wear that jewelry outside, but if you were to be killed by a crook, the twins wouldn't get to know you."

"Don't know me now," Sophie muttered. "That blasted woman won't let me near them."

"How about a compromise," Vicky suggested. "You agree not to wear the jewelry outside the house, and James will instruct Nanny to let you see the twins whenever you want except during nap time. Is that all right, James?"

"Yes," James agreed promptly. "You promise, Aunt Sophie, and I'll speak to Nanny."

"Oh, all right," Sophie conceded. "I still think

you're being paranoid, but if it means that much to you, dear boy, I won't do it anymore.''

''Thank you.'' James gave Sophie a smile that expanded to include Vicky, who felt warmed by his obvious approval.

Unfortunately, their feeling of companionship was abruptly shattered when they walked into the house and discovered Esmee standing in the hallway holding a manila envelope in front of her like a sword.

''Aha! There you are.'' Esmee glared at Vicky.

Vicky suppressed the fatuous impulse to deny that she was there and pasted a polite smile on her face instead. It was an effort. Not only did she resent the woman's breaking up their happy mood, but the gloating expression on Esmee Defoe's face made her very uneasy.

''James, I have news for you, which, if you had listened to me in the first place, you would already know,'' Esmee announced.

''Esmee, I am not in the mood for dramatics,'' James said discouragingly.

''Dramatics!'' Esmee's voice rose to a very unattractive shriek.

''Or histrionics,'' James muttered under his breath.

''Do you know who that woman is?'' She gestured melodramatically toward Vicky, and Vicky felt her stomach contract with sudden alarm.

Please don't let her have found out who I am before I can tell him. Vicky muttered a silent prayer.

Heaven was deaf to her plea.

''This woman is no relative of yours. She isn't even English. Her family immigrated to America from Italy! Her name is really Sutton, and she only pretended to be someone called Lascoe so she could claim to be related to you and worm her way into Thayer House.''

''To steal the silver, no doubt,'' Sophie said with a disgusted look at Esmee.

Esmee ignored her. ''Read this, James.'' She tried to give him the manila envelope she was waving about. ''I hired a private detective to look into her background.''

Vicky finally found the courage to look at James, and her heart sank at the expression in his eyes. They were cold. Cold and withdrawn and unforgiving.

Without a word to either the triumphant Esmee or the stricken Vicky, he turned on his heel and left.

Vicky watched him walk away from her, feeling as if her heart would break.

Chapter Eleven

James carefully closed the study door behind him, feeling as if he would shatter into a million irretrievable pieces at the slightest noise. He removed his shaking fingers from the brass doorknob and stiffly walked across the room, drawn by the warmth of the late-evening sunlight pouring in through the windows. He felt cold. Icy cold all the way through.

Blindly he stared at the peaceful scene outside the window as he struggled to get a grip on the raging pain of Vicky's betrayal.

One thing about you, Thayer, he berated himself, you certainly are consistent in your taste in women. First, Romayne and now Vicky. Both had wanted what he possessed and not what he was. And he'd been dumb enough to believe both of them.

But Vicky's betrayal hurt so much more. He sucked in his breath at the pain slicing through him. It felt as if some malicious entity were busily rearranging his body on the cellular level.

He slammed his fist down on his desk in sudden frustration. Why had Vicky lied to him? And why the hell did it hurt so much that she had? It shouldn't. He'd only known her a short time. How could her betrayal hurt so much?

It hurt because he loved her. The appalling truth welled up out of his subconscious and then ebbed away, leaving a sense of devastation in its wake.

"I love her." He mumbled the idea aloud and found it sounded as appalling spoken as thought.

James clenched his fists in impotent frustration. He wanted to smash something. To get roaring drunk. To do something violent to relieve his frustrations. He couldn't. He didn't have the luxury of indulging himself. Not only would it frighten his aunt, but he had the twins to think of. A father who solved his problems by violence, even if it was only directed against things, or who drowned his problems in alcohol, even temporarily, was not a proper role model.

James swung around and stared blindly at the wall behind him. He studied it for a long moment as if seeking inspiration from its cream walls. He didn't find any. He couldn't seem to get past the pain filling him. The pain of Vicky's betrayal.

Now what? he wondered. Did the woman he loved even exist? Or had he somehow created someone because...

Because why? he wondered uncertainly. He hadn't been looking for a woman to fall in love with. On the contrary, he hadn't wanted to get emotionally involved with anyone. He'd been there and done that. Once had been more than enough in his estimation. No, he hadn't set himself up for this pain. Not consciously, at any rate.

But it really didn't matter why or how he had fallen in love with her. He released his breath in a long, dispirited sigh. What mattered was that he was in love with Vicky Las—no, with Vicky Sutton, and he was going to have to deal with it. Somehow.

"You'll be leaving now, I assume." Esmee gave Vicky a self-satisfied smirk that Vicky longed to smack off the woman's face. The very strength of the compulsion shook Vicky. She wasn't a violent person and yet the thought of physically attacking Esmee Defoe gave her nothing but a surge of primitive pleasure.

"I mean, now that James knows who you really are," Esmee continued smugly, seemingly oblivious to the violent emotions raging through Vicky. "I'll drive you to the train station," she continued. "You can have your luggage sent on later. That way you won't have to face the family again."

Vicky sucked in her breath, her anger at Esmee temporarily eclipsed by the pain she felt at the soul-shattering thought of never seeing James again.

"The family?" Sophie's imperious voice came from behind Vicky, making her jump. In the confusion Vicky had totally forgotten about Sophie.

"And who are you to speak of what the Thayer family wants?" Sophie glared at Esmee. "I have put up with your appalling lack of manners because your grandmother was my dearest friend, and I felt I owed it to her memory to give you every chance to change. But enough is enough!"

"You're just an old woman who's long outlived her usefulness," Esmee spat.

Vicky took a protective step toward Sophie's frail figure, but to her amazement Sophie seemed to take on added strength while she watched. As if the spirits of her long-dead ancestors were lending her stature.

"Get out of this house." Sophie delivered the words dispassionately. "You have done what you came to do, which was to cause trouble. But I rather think you have greatly miscalculated."

Sophie sent a speculative look at Vicky that confused her. "On several fronts."

"I'll go for now, but when James and I are married…"

"James will never marry you," Sophie announced. "He doesn't even much like you. Now get out before I call Beech and have you shown out."

Esmee's face turned a dull red and with a final, frustrated glare, which she divided equally between Vicky and Sophie, turned on her heel and stomped out.

"I have often wondered if her mother played her father false, because I find it impossible to believe that she is Emma's granddaughter," Sophie said thoughtfully.

"Um…Sophie," Vicky said slowly, not sure if Sophie understood that she really had lied to both her and James. "Esmee wasn't wrong. I'm not really Vicky Lascoe. I'm Vicky Sutton."

"What's in a name?" Sophie demanded. "You're still the same gel you were before, ain't you?"

"Well, yes, but…" Vicky bit her lip. Sophie might think a name didn't matter, but James most emphatically did.

James, with the memory of his ex-wife's betrayals, would view her lie in a much less benevolent light. In all likelihood, he'd demand that she leave. Fear spurted through her, threatening to completely immobilize her. Desperately she tried to wall it off so she could think.

So she could try to decide what to do. What she could do. All she was certain of was that she felt as if something vital had been torn out of her when James had turned and walked away from her. She felt as if she were hemorrhaging her life's blood from a gaping wound.

"But how can I make him understand?" Vicky muttered her thoughts aloud.

"Don't know," Sophie's answered promptly. "But I do know that dithering around out here with me ain't going to fix anything."

"No," Vicky conceded, knowing that she was going to have to confront James and yet terrified to do so. He hadn't said anything directly to her. He hadn't told her that he despised her. He hadn't said he never wanted to see her again. He hadn't threatened to try to block her seeing their children. He hadn't told her to get out of his house. Yet.

But if she sought him out, he'd have the opportunity to say all of those things and probably a whole lot more. She didn't think she could bear to hear it. She loved him so much. Wanted him so much that to have him reject her...

She closed her eyes against the jagged pain at the very thought.

"Ain't going to solve anything standing there looking like you just lost your last friend, gel," Sophie prodded her. "I thought you modern women were up to anything. Where's your gumption?"

A ragged chuckle choked on the sob that escaped Vicky. "I never had all that much gumption to start with, Sophie. But you're right. I have to do something."

"So, go do it," Sophie encouraged her. "Time things were settled, anyway,"

Vicky gave Sophie a sickly smile and headed for James's study. She assumed that was where he had gone, since it seemed to be his normal bolt-hole.

Vicky paused in front of the study's mahogany door and swallowed, trying to settle her churning stomach. It didn't work. Giving up, she raised one hand and gave a tentative knock on the door.

"Yes?" James's deep voice from behind the closed door did not sound welcoming, and Vicky felt her spirit quail.

Confidence, she told herself. What's the worst thing that can happen if you continue with your present course of action? Trying to use one of the techniques from her course was a mistake. The appalling scenarios that immediately leaped to mind almost paralyzed her.

Determinedly sweeping them away, she forced herself to open the door and step inside.

Her eyes instinctively homed in on James. He was sitting behind his desk eyeing her coldly.

"What do you want?" he demanded.

What did she want? The words floated through her mind raising all sorts of possibilities. For him to listen to her. To tell her he understood. To tell her it didn't matter. To tell her that he loved her…. Concentrate on the possible, she told herself.

"I want to—" she groped for words "—to explain why…"

"Why you lied to me?"

"Yes, I lied," Vicky admitted. "I was going to let Ms Lascoe come, but I found I couldn't bear to send someone else to see my children. They were my children." Her voice rose on the strength of her feelings.

"I had a right to see them. To love them, and you were being so…damned unreasonable about it.

"So at the last minute I decided to pretend to be Ms. Lascoe."

"You lied to me," he repeated.

"I lied, but not to you. Not to you personally." Vicky rushed on when he opened his mouth to argue. "I didn't know you then. You were simply the man who was the father of my children. The man who was trying to prevent me from seeing them. You weren't real in any sense of the word. There wasn't anything personal in my lying to you."

James forced himself to look out the window instead of continuing to look at her. Despite knowing that she had lied to him, that she had played him for a sucker, he still wanted to take her in his arms. He wanted to kiss her and wipe away her fearful expression. His mind might tell him she didn't need protecting—*he* was the one who needed protecting from her machinations—but his emotions didn't believe it. They reacted to her on a level that had nothing to do with common sense. Or even with self-preservation.

"You claim you didn't tell me in the beginning because you wanted access to the twins," he said. "But once you got it, why didn't you tell me? Why continue the farce? Surely you must have realized that I…liked you."

Vicky stared into his pain-filled features and felt an answering twist of pain lance through her. She had caused his pain. That she hadn't meant to do it was no excuse. Her actions, her cowardly dithering over telling him who she really was had led directly to this.

And since she had caused James's pain, it was up to her to relieve it. At least, as far as she was able. And the only way she could see was to tell him the truth. All of it. Mentally she cringed at the thought of opening herself up to more rejection. But her own feelings didn't matter. She had to try to right the wrong she had done. She loved him far too much not to.

"I didn't tell you the truth because I was afraid to," she began.

"Was I such an ogre?" he demanded in frustration.

"No, it would have been easier if you had been. Then I wouldn't have felt so guilty about lying. In the beginning I was afraid to tell you the truth because I thought you'd tell me to get out before I had a chance to get to know the twins. And then I...I fell in love with you and was even more afraid of your reaction," she blurted out.

Vicky stared fearfully at his dear face, desperately trying to read some response to her words. She couldn't. His features might have been carved in stone. Only his eyes were alive, and they seemed to glow with some violent emotion.

"Dammit, don't compound the lie!" he yelled at her.

Vicky inadvertently stepped back, pushed away by the force of his rage.

"I'm not lying. And I certainly didn't want to be in love with you. It was a disaster as far as I was concerned. But you were so..." She gestured impotently, at a loss for words. How could she explain why she had fallen in love with him, when she didn't understand it herself? It had just happened because he was who he was and she was who she was and...

She sighed in defeat. Maybe she ought to blame the whole thing on fate.

"You don't have to lie," he said. "I'll give you what you want."

Vicky felt her heart leap, and she stared at him with sudden hope.

"I'll let you have joint custody of the twins if you agree not to take them out of England."

Vicky blinked, trying to process what he'd actually said. James was offering her joint custody of the twins. That was good. She wanted that. But the twins were no longer her only goal.

"Thank you, I accept your offer," she finally said, "but the twins aren't the main issue at the moment. They may have been what originally set everything in motion. But now this is about..." She was going to say us, but thought better of it. She didn't really know that this was about them. All she knew for certain was that she loved James Thayer. Exactly how he felt about her was still a mystery. Even his violent reaction to her deception could be more about bad memories of his first wife's lies than a reaction to her personally.

"I don't know if this is about me or you or us," she burst out saying in frustration. "All I know is that I am madly in love with a man that at the moment I want to smack upside the head for being so blasted dense."

"You think you love me?" James said, wanting more than anything he'd ever wanted to believe her. If he was wrong this time it would destroy him. He loved her so much and if she betrayed him...

"I *know* I love you," Vicky corrected. "After the fiasco of my first marriage, I know the difference."

"You could just be saying that to get the twins." He muttered his thoughts aloud. Caring too much led to pain, and he didn't think there was any other way to love Vicky but too much. The very intensity of her personality demanded it.

"I already have the twins," she said grittily. "You just gave me joint custody. Remember?"

Yes, he remembered. He'd expected her to eagerly accept his offer and then leave. But she hadn't. It was almost as if she didn't care. No, that wasn't quite right, he decided as he studied the signs of strain on her delicately molded features. She cared very deeply about something, and the only thing left was him.

A sudden burst of excitement fountained through him. She must be telling him the truth. There really was no reason to lie to him anymore. As inexplicable as he found it, she really did love him.

Suddenly unable to stand the width of the desk between them, he rounded it. Reaching for her, he pulled her into his arms, and for a moment it was sufficient to simply feel her slender body pressed the length of his. To absorb the scent of her.

Vicky wrapped her arms around his broad chest, trying to get closer to him. "Does this mean you believe me?" she finally gathered the courage to ask.

James loosened his grasp and, cupping her chin in his hand, tilted her face up so that he could relish the sight of her.

"Yes, I believe you. It also means that I love you to distraction and intend to marry you as soon as it can be arranged." He stared down at her lips and felt longing twist through him.

"Yes, please," she said simply, and tugged his head down to hers.

Vicky felt his lips cover hers with a supreme feeling of rightness. For the first time in her life she no longer regretted the pain of her first marriage. It had turned her into the person she was today. It had, in a strange way, brought her to James and, above all, it had shown her just how rare and precious the love she had for him was. Then she stopped thinking and simply felt. And it felt very good.

* * * * *

Silhouette Romance presents tales of
enchanted love and things beyond explanation
in the heartwarming series,

Soulmates

Couples destined for each other are brought
together by the powerful magic of love....

The second time around
brings an unexpected suitor, in
THE WISH
by Diane Pershing (on sale April 2003)

The power of love battles a medieval spell, in
THE KNIGHT'S KISS
by Nicole Burnham (on sale May 2003)

Soulmates

Some things are meant to be....

*Available at
your favorite retail outlet.*

CATCHING THE CROWN

Secrets and passion abound
as the royals reclaim their throne!

Bestselling author

RAYE MORGAN

brings you a special installment
of her new miniseries

ROYAL
NIGHTS

On sale May 2003

When a terrifying act of sabotage nearly takes the life of Prince Damian
of Nabotavia, he is plunged into a world of darkness. Hell-bent on
discovering who tried to kill him, the battle-scarred prince searches
tirelessly for the truth. The unwavering support of Sara, his fearless
therapist, is the only light in Damian's bleak world. But will revealing
his most closely guarded secret throw Sara into the line of fire?

Don't miss the other books in this exciting miniseries:

JACK AND THE PRINCESS (Silhouette Romance #1655)
On sale April 2003

BETROTHED TO THE PRINCE (Silhouette Romance #1667)
On sale June 2003

COUNTERFEIT PRINCESS (Silhouette Romance #1672)
On sale July 2003

Available wherever Silhouette books are sold.

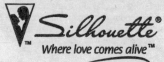

Silhouette®

Where love comes alive™

SILHOUETTE *Romance*

COMING NEXT MONTH

#1654 DADDY ON THE DOORSTEP—Judy Christenberry

Despite their fairy-tale courtship, Andrea's marriage to Nicholas Avery was struggling. But when a torrential downpour left them stranded, Andrea had one last chance to convince her emotionally scarred husband that he was the perfect husband and—surprise!—daddy!

#1655 JACK AND THE PRINCESS—Raye Morgan

Catching the Crown

Princess Karina Roseanova was expected to marry an appropriate suitor—but found herself *much* more attracted to her sexy bodyguard, Jack Santini. Smitten, Jack knew that a relationship with the adorable princess was a bad idea. So when the job was over, he would walk away…right?

#1656 THE RANCHER'S HAND-PICKED BRIDE—
Elizabeth August

Jess Logan was long, lean, sexy as sin—and not in the market for marriage. But his great-grandmother was determined to see him settled, so she enlisted Gwen Murphy's help. Jess hadn't counted on Gwen's matchmaking resolve or the havoc she wreaked on his heart. Could the match for Jess be…Gwen?

#1657 THE WISH—Diane Pershing

Soulmates

Shy bookstore owner Gerri Conklin's dream date was a total disaster! She wished to relive the week, vowing to get it right. But when her wish was granted, she found herself choosing between the man she *thought* she loved—and the strong, silent rancher who stole his way into her heart!

#1658 A WHOLE NEW MAN—Roxann Delaney

Image consultant Lizzie Edwards wanted a stable home for her young daughter, and that didn't include Hank Davis, the handsome man who'd hired her to instruct him about the finer things in life. But her new client left her weak-kneed, and soon she was mixing business with pleasure….

#1659 HE'S STILL THE ONE—Cheryl Kushner

Zoe Russell returned to Riverbend and made a big splash in police chief Ryan O'Conner's life—ending up in jail! Formerly best friends, they hadn't spoken in years. As they worked to repair their relationship, sparks flew, the air sizzled…but *when* did friends start kissing like *that*?

SRCNM0303